MULTITUDES

MULTITUDES

Eleven Stories

LUCY CALDWELL

FABER & FABER

First published in 2016
by Faber & Faber Limited
Bloomsbury House
74–77 Great Russell Street
London WC1B 3DA

Typeset by Reality Premedia Services Pvt. Ltd.
Printed and bound in the UK by CPI Group (UK) Ltd, Croydon CR0 4YY

'Escape Routes' was shortlisted for the 2012 BBC International Short Story Award
and was published in the award anthology (Comma Press, 2012); 'Inextinguishable'
was commissioned and broadcast by BBC Radio 3 (February 2013); 'Through the
Wardrobe' was commissioned and broadcast by BBC Radio 4 (November 2013);
'Poison' was published in *Belfast Noir*, ed. Adrian McKinty and Stuart Neville
(Akashic Books, 2014); 'Killing Time' won the Commonwealth Writers' Prize
(Canada and Europe) and was published in *All Over Ireland: New Irish Short Stories*,
ed. Deirdre Madden (Faber & Faber, 2015); 'Multitudes' was published in *The Long
Gaze Back: An Anthology of Irish Women Writers*, ed. Sinéad Gleeson (New Island,
2015).

A CIP record for this book is available from the British Library.

ISBN 978-0-571-31350-1

2 4 6 8 10 9 7 5 3 1

Ain't nothing but a stranger in this world
I'm nothing but a stranger in this world
I got a home on high
In another land
So far away
So far away

Van Morrison, 'Astral Weeks'

For William
and everything that brought you, us, here, now

Contents

MULTITUDES

The Ally Ally O

THE BIG SHIP SAILS ON THE ALLY ALLY O, your youngest sister is singing, the Ally ally o, the Ally ally o, the big ship sails on the Ally ally o on the last day of September. Al-ly ally o, she belts out each time she gets to the chorus, Al-ly ally o, al-ly ally ally o-o-o.

You want to shout at her to shut up. You put your thumb over your right ear and lean your forehead against the window so you can concentrate. You think you're on the road that leads to the Ice Bowl. But you can't be sure. It's raining outside, and the smear of raindrops on the window makes it impossible to read street names when they flash past. Besides, everywhere looks different now you're playing the game. Familiar places appear at unexpected times, as if distances have somehow gone wrong, or they fail to appear at all, because you've turned off the wrong road too early, or onto the right road too late. You used to love the Getting Lost game. When your mum suggested playing it, you and your middle sister, then your only sister, would be beside yourselves with excitement. Once you ended up at the Pickie Fun Park and pedalled all around the lake on a giant plastic swan. Another time there was a carnival at Lady Dixon Park with helium balloons and face-painting. You a tiger; your sister a butterfly. The warm, waxy feeling of the colour on your cheeks.

Your mum must have planned it, you realise now, somehow steered your choices. You don't think she has a plan today. How can she: she was right in the middle of the ironing, huge drifts of still-damp bedsheets, a cassoulet half-done on the stove and the radio droning when she said, I need to get out of here. The three of you, chasing each other round the dining-room table and out through the conservatory and back, stopped and looked.

The Captain says it'll neverever do, neverever do, neverever do, sings your youngest sister, more hyper with every passing minute.

Shut up, you scream inside your head. Shut up.

Your whole body feels hot and damp. Your leggings are made out of wool, and they're itching your legs. You press your forehead into the window.

The road to the Ice Bowl: it has to be. Maybe you're going to Indiana Land, the rope bridges and the ball pit and the Freefall. For a moment you feel the sensation of sitting on the edge of it, legs dangling, arms crossed over your chest, before the attendant yells at you to go, go, go.

But your mum said she'd never take you there again after the rumours there was a rat in the ball pit. It was meant to be living off spilled Slush Puppies and leftover chips. It was a monster rat, a mutant. It was a whole family of rats. It bit a baby in the soft-play area. Dragged it under the plastic

2

balls and gnawed its eyes out. Even the mums were talking about it at the school gates.

The Captain says it'll neverever do on the last day of September. Al-ly ally o, al-ly ally o, al-ly ally ally o-o-o—

Your youngest sister breaks off. Mum, she says. What does Ally ally o mean?

Well, says your mum. I'd say it's the Atlantic Ocean. 'Ally' for Atlantic and 'O' for ocean. And the big ship's the *Titanic*. Left at these lights or straight on?

Straight on, your middle sister says.

Okey-doke, says your mum, and accelerates.

Pedal to the metal, flat to the mat, your middle sister says, imitating your dad, and your mum laughs. For the flash of a second, you hate your sister.

It's not the *Titanic*, you hear yourself saying. The *Titanic* sailed from Belfast on the second of April and from Southampton on the tenth of April at noon. You can't help adding, It might be the SS *Arctic*, though. The SS *Arctic* sank at the end of September. It was the fastest, most famous ship of its day, but it collided with the French steamer *Vesta* off the coast of Newfoundland and almost all on board perished.

Your mum glances at you in the rear-view mirror. Is that from that book? she says.

No, you say, too quickly. From school.

Your face is hot with the lie, and you're sure she can see it. It's true, you say. After the SS *Arctic* the shipping lines promised to reform their safety provision but the *Titanic*'s tragedy was that she was considered by all to be unsinkable.

Mum! your middle sister says.

Oh sorry, your mum says. Never mind, look, there's another set of lights coming up ahead.

I want to choose, your youngest sister says. How come I never get to choose?

You do get to choose.

No, I never.

Girls, your mum says. Then she says to your youngest sister, Okay, straight on or right?

Your youngest sister wriggles in her booster seat and claps with glee. Right, she says. I mean straight on. No, right.

Are you sure? your mum says.

Yes. No . . . yes. Stop laughing at me. Mum, tell her to stop laughing at me.

I'm not laughing at you.

Yes, you are. You're laughing inside your face.

Laughing inside my face?

You are.

Girls, I'm warning you.

I didn't do anything.

Yes she did!

Right, your mum says. I'm turning right. She flicks on the indicator and pulls into the lane for turning right. Your mum's voice is suddenly too bright again. I need to get out of here. Get your shoes on, all of you. I've had enough of this.

Your whole body is itching now.

The Captain of the SS *Arctic* was Captain James Luce, you say. He went down with his ship standing atop a wooden box, but in a quirk of fate it bobbed to the surface, and he

4

clung on until he was rescued two days later. His sickly son, Willie, however, perished. All the children on board were drowned, and all the women too, because the panicking crew had scrambled into the lifeboats themselves.

You're banned from reading that book, your middle sister says. Isn't she, Mum?

A, I'm banned from reading it before bed. You can feel your voice trembling. And B, I wasn't reading, I was reciting.

Mum? your middle sister says.

You make your eyes meet your mum's in the mirror. You can't work out her expression. You used to think she really did have eyes in the back of her head: that was how she knew what you and your sister were up to. It was almost a disappointment to realise how it worked.

You know all that by heart, your mum says.

You can't tell if it's a question or a warning. Yes, you say.

You wait for your mum to say something, but she doesn't, and your middle sister, who's twisted round to look at you through the gap in the seats, turns back with a huff of disappointment.

The World's Greatest Ever Disasters! You bought it with your birthday book tokens, and at first your parents laughed at your choice. The *Titanic* is in there, and the SS *Arctic*. The *Hindenburg*, 6 May 1937. The explosion of the ICMESA reactor in Meda, Italy, on the tenth of July 1976, which led to a cloud of dioxin, one of the most toxic chemicals known to man, being released into the atmosphere. The Cocoanut Grove nightclub fire on the twenty-eighth of November 1942, which started when a teenage busboy tried to turn back on a lightbulb that had been unscrewed by a couple wanting to kiss in the dark.

On the blank pages at the end you've made a secret list of world disasters that have happened since the book was published. Only the very worst ones make it in there, the ones where hundreds of people die at a time, where whole cities are wiped out in one fell swoop, whole swathes of the world destroyed forever. Typhoons, monsoons, earthquakes, mud slides. Stunt planes colliding at air shows and smashing into the crowd. Drilling platforms in the North Sea exploding. Toxic gas leaks. On the twenty-sixth of April 1986, the meltdown of the fourth reactor at the Chernobyl plant. There was radiation detected over Scotland within hours. On a clear Sunday you can see the coast of Scotland from Crawfordsburn, as if it's no distance at all. Your most recent addition, 24 March 1989, the *Exxon Valdez* oil spill in the Prince William Sound. You keep the book hidden at the bottom of the piano stool and only take it out when you really have to. Sometimes it's a relief to know it's there. Sometimes you wish your parents would ban it entirely.

The road is narrowing as it climbs into the hills. The rain is coming down more heavily now, lashing against the right-hand side of the car. You can feel the car shake, as if it's trembling.

Are we lost yet? your youngest sister says.

I think we might be, says your mum.

It's only a game, you tell yourself. It's only a stupid game. You're in the countryside proper now. Hedges and mud and fields. The road twists and turns, climbing higher and higher.

We're going to have a great view of the city in a minute girls, your mum says.

How do you know? your middle sister says, accusingly. If you don't know where we are, then how do you know where we'll be?

Sorry, your mum says, but she catches your eye in the rear-view mirror and you know it's deliberate.

The car rounds a bend, and your mum slows right down. There you go, she says.

You crane to look out her side of the car.

What is it? your youngest sister says. Where?

I can see some cows, your middle sister says, still sulking, and some fields and some rain. Big wow.

On a good day, your mum says, the view from here is the best view in the world. On a good day, you can see all of the city, Samson and Goliath standing over the docks, and Queen's Island, and all the way across the lough to Cave Hill and Divis and the Black Mountain, all of it, as if you could just scoop it all up and hold it in the palm of your hand.

I thought you said you didn't know where we were, your middle sister mutters.

I didn't know until we got here that this was where we were going, says your mum.

The Black Mountain, your youngest sister says. Have I ever been there?

No, says your mum. No, you haven't.

Why not?

Well, says your mum, I don't know my way around that part of the city.

Can we go there one day, but?

One day, says your mum.

For a moment, the only noise is the click-click of the indicator and the windscreen wipers going back and forth. Your youngest sister doesn't know yet that 'one day' means not ever. She doesn't know that there are places that you never ever go, not on purpose and not even by accident. One wrong turn, one wrong consonant; that's all it takes.

When I first came over, your mum says suddenly, your dad drove me up here at dusk, to watch the lights come on all over the city. That's when I thought, Yes, I could live here after all.

You always tell us to grow up and get away, you say.

Do I? your mum says. No I don't.

You do.

You do, Mum, your middle sister chimes in.

Well. I suppose I do, sometimes. Maybe all parents do. We probably don't mean it literally. We probably just mean, make your world a better place.

She sits for a moment. Then she shakes her head and sighs, checks the mirrors and turns the indicator off, starts driving again.

Are we going home now? your youngest sister says.

Your mum looks at the dashboard clock. Seventeen minutes past four, it says.

I don't know, your mum says. Do you think we can find our way back?

Your youngest sister drums her heels against the seat in pleasure. Al-ly ally o! she screeches.

Oh not that song again, your middle sister says. She's like a broken record, isn't she, Mum?

I am not, your youngest sister says. Mum, tell her to say sorry.

She didn't mean it, your mum says. Did I ever tell you, we used to sing that song when I was a little girl?

Really? says your youngest sister, forgetting to be offended.

I always used to assume it was about the *Titanic*, says your mum. But I stand corrected.

Did you really used to sing it? your youngest sister says.

We had a game that went along with it. You all held hands and wove in and out of each other's arms, then tumbled down in a heap at the end. I haven't thought about that in years. We used to play it in our street, a dozen of us at a time.

In Manchester? says your middle sister.

In Manchester, your mum says.

When you were a little girl before you grew up and met Dad and moved here and had us, says your youngest sister.

Yes, your mum says. I suppose that's about the sum of it.

The road takes you past Four Winds, where your piano teacher used to live, and then joins the big dual carriageway. Who can get us home from here? your mum says, and your youngest sister says, Me! Me!, and your middle sister says, Boring, it's just straight all the way now.

Your youngest sister is no longer singing, but the song plays on a loop in your head.

We all dip our heads in the deep blue sea.

It wouldn't be blue, you think. There would be thick walls of grey-green fog and the waters black, choppy with rolling white-capped waves, the temperature reaching freezing. Huge jagged dirty-looking icebergs looming out of nowhere. Your dad says the joke about the *Titanic* is, She was fine when she left us.

With the heel of your hand you rub a patch of the window clear of condensation, but there's hardly anything to see, the bright moons of oncoming headlights, the red of tail lights, the rain.

Thirteen

ON THE FIRST OF JULY, SUSAN CLARKE and her family move to London to start a new life. They've had enough is what Susan's mum says. She just can't take it any more. 'This country,' she says to my mum.

'This country,' my mum says back to her, and neither of them says anything else.

Susan and I have been best friends since nursery school – since before nursery school, we always say to each other, in actual fact since Mothers and Toddlers in the hall of the Methodist church on the corner where her street meets mine. I don't remember that far back, only vaguely – plastic cups of orange squash and dusty, frilled-edge biscuits, the smell of floor polish – but I can't remember, let alone imagine, life without her.

We cry and hug and hug again and promise we'll write to each other every other day, and all summer we do, mine big packets of letters with wax seals on the back of the envelope and hers folded up like origami fortune-tellers, a different private joke written under each pointed flap.

My dad and I look up Ealing on a map, where her dad

comes from, where they've gone back to. On the corner of their new street is a little park called Haven Green which I misread for weeks as Heaven.

Then September comes and Susan's letters change. I read them over and over, trying to work out what's wrong. They are as detailed as ever: more detailed, in fact, because she's started her new school and has so much to tell me. But they feel somehow thinner, rushed. She stops making origami and writes on ordinary paper instead, ripped from a fileblock and folded unevenly. She's just busy, my mum says. But then her letters start to tail off. Twice a week instead of three times, then once. She stops reminding me who all the new people are and so her stories get confusing, then impossible to follow. When I write back asking questions she forgets to answer them. I don't have anything new to tell her. Everything's just the same as it always has been, only without her.

I spend hours each night trying to shape the day into stories to make her laugh. What Mr McNeill said in Technology. How someone saw Miss Rice in town holding hands with a man who had a shaved head and DM boots. When I run out of things to say, I write again about the old things. About the night before our Eleven Plus results when we had sausage and chips in the upstairs room of the Silver Leaf café then went to the Strand to see *My Girl* and cried so much when Thomas J. died we started laughing. About the mood rings from Fresh Garbage in town we swapped the week after. About the time we nicked Michael's Game Gear and spent a whole weekend playing

Sonic the Hedgehog until we worked out how to defeat Dr Robotnik and finish the game, and how raging he was that we'd done it first. I write about the Easters and half-terms we've gone down South in my parents' caravan, the two of us sleeping side by side on the sofa that pulls out into a double bed. I write about the afternoons we spent phoning Long Wave Radio Atlantic 252 to win the dancing Fruitini can, which still sits on my window sill, and I write passages in the secret language that we made up.

My letters get longer, and hers start to say, I'll write back properly next time.

I turn thirteen. Susan phones up and sings 'Happy Birthday' down the phone. Her voice sounds different now: rounder, louder, as if there's more room in her mouth. She says things like 'cool' and 'way to go'. For the first time ever, I don't know what to say to her and wish I'd made a list, the way we used to do in case a boy rang up to ask us out. After the third or fourth silence, she says, 'Well, gotta go,' and it's almost a relief. I've been secretly hoping she'll be there for my birthday party on the Saturday night, even though she's said she can't be, but when I hang up the phone I know for sure she's not coming.

My thirteenth birthday party is the worst night of my life. I haven't known who to invite and I've invited most of the class. My parents have pushed the living-room furniture up against the walls to make space, cooked pizzas and oven chips, lined up big bottles of Shloer. At the last minute, my mum carries in a chocolate cake from the bakery on Bloomfield Avenue, decorated to look like a handbag. 'We were going to bring it in halfway through,' she says, 'but we don't want to embarrass you in front of all your friends, so here you go.'

'Wow,' I say, 'thanks,' and I try to look grateful.

'D'you know,' she says after a while, and smoothes my ponytail, 'every party I've ever had I've worried about nobody coming.'

'Yeah,' I say. There's no way of explaining that while I'm dreading people not coming, I'm dreading them arriving even more. At last the doorbell goes. 'You see?' says my mum.

'Have a blast,' my dad says, and winks to show they won't mind the noise, and they go upstairs as they've promised.

About half the class turns up, boys as well as girls, and enough people that it's not a disaster. But after the pizza and cake have been demolished and the boys have got bored of chucking leftover chips at each other, everyone decides to play Truth or Dare. They say I have to go first because I'm the birthday girl, and Vicky Shaw makes a show of smirking at her clique. Then she asks, 'Have you ever seen anybody?'

I can feel everyone looking at me. Someone sniggers.

'We're waiting,' says Alison Reid.

'Did you not hear the question?' says Vicky Shaw. 'I'll ask it one more time. Have . . . you . . . ever . . . seen . . . anybody?'

'Dare,' I say, and everyone cracks up.

'All right then,' Vicky Shaw shouts over them, 'all right then, here's your dare,' and they all go quiet again, waiting to see what it'll be. 'As your dare,' she says, 'as your dare, you have to see all the boys in this room.'

'Wise up,' I say.

'You have to,' Alison Reid says.

'You don't have a choice,' Emma J chimes in.

Vicky Shaw swishes her hair. She's loving this. Everyone is loving this. 'I'm not going to,' I say, lamely.

'Why not? Are you a lesbo?' she crows. 'Were you and Susan Clarke lesbos together?'

At that the whole room goes mad with wolf whistles and clapping and cries of 'Gross,' and 'Yeooooo,' and 'Lesbo!'

'No,' I say, 'wise up, of course not.' My voice sounds hoarse. 'That's disgusting,' I say.

Last year, a rumour started that Helen Russell from the year above was looking at other girls in the showers after PE, and for a whole term people stuck sanitary towels on the back of her blazer and Pamela Anderson posters on the door of her locker. We had a Junior School Assembly about bullying, but it didn't change anything, and eventually her parents took her out of school. You saw them in Supermac sometimes, Helen Russell trailing after her mum, staring at the floor in case she saw someone she knew.

I don't have a choice. 'Fine then,' I say, 'I'll do the dare.'

They blindfold me with someone's scarf, and the boys spin an empty Shloer bottle to decide the order they'll go in. The first kiss isn't too bad, pepperoni breath and dry chapped lips and then it's over. The second is wet and spitty, like being kissed by a Labrador. The third goes on for so long people start slow-clapping. The fourth boy thrusts his tongue so hard I almost gag. The cheering is getting louder. Someone gulders, 'Get her bucked!' and for a few seconds it becomes a chant. Then the fifth boy grabs my shoulders and shoves me onto my knees and up against his crotch. When I realise what's happening and manage to wrench away and rip off the scarf, everyone goes mental, howling and whistling and punching the air and yelling. It's Paul Forrester – fat Paul Forrester, who got stuck halfway up the ropes in PE last year and started crying in front of everyone – and as he zips up his flies and pushes his glasses back on his fat sweaty face, Andy Milford gives him a high five and says, 'Nice one, big fella.'

My eyes are stinging, and I blink furiously and try not to cry, tell myself I must not cry because they are all watching me to see if I will, and I realise that I haven't got a single friend in the whole room.

After that, I put off writing to Susan. At night, I can't seem to sleep. When I close my eyes, I can't get rid of the memory of Paul Forrester's dick: how it had taken me a few seconds to realise what it was, how it had been soft and squashy and musty-smelling at first and then a tremor had run through it and it had twitched through his boxer shorts against my mouth. I lie awake and stare at the glow-in-the-dark stars on my ceiling.

A week passes, and then another. Susan sends me a postcard saying 'Troc Till You Drop!' On the back she has written,

London is soooo cool. I am happier here than I have ever been in my entire life. It's such a relief not always to be the only one!!

I can't think what to write back.

It goes all around school what happened at my party. The story gets more and more exaggerated until one day a group of girls from the year above ask if it's true I gave a boy a blow job in front of everyone and if it is true I'm such a dirty wee hoor.

At break and lunch I sit alone now. Any chance I had of making new friends is gone. No one wants to risk being seen with me. When we need to split into pairs in class, I end up with Jacqueline Dunne, the other Norma in the class. No one likes Jacqueline because she's so two-faced. She's one of the biggest slabbers in the year and yet she's always the one squealing to the teachers. But she's all I've got. She starts asking me to stay over at hers some Saturday night so we can go down Cairnburn like Vicky Shaw and Andy Milford and all the others do now, and every time I make excuses. I'd rather have no friends at all than have Jacqueline Dunne as a best friend.

But one Friday night I'm watching TV with my parents when my dad says, 'What do your friends do at the weekends, ey?' He says it too casually, and he doesn't look at my mum as he says it, which is how I know they've been discussing it.

I freeze. 'They just,' I say. 'You know.'

'Why don't you ask a friend to stay the night?' my mum says.

My heart starts thumping. They have no idea about my birthday party. They have no idea about anything. So many times, I've felt the longing to tell them everything rise up inside me and spread in my chest like a bruise. I stop myself with the thought of how sad they'd be, how furious, and, worst of all, how extra-specially nice they'd be to me. I know, too, that in private they'd blame themselves for insisting I had a party.

I'd cried and cried when Susan left, and at first my mum had said things like, 'You'll make other friends,' and, 'Of course people will want to sit with you,' and, 'Just be yourself.' When she came up with the idea of a big birthday party, she was so delighted I didn't know how to say no.

'Actually,' I hear myself blurt out, 'Jacqueline Dunne said did I want to sleep over at hers tomorrow.'

'That's great,' my dad says.

'Of course you can,' says my mum. 'You should have said before. We've been so worried you were lonely.'

'No,' I say. I feel my face heating up, so I stand and say, 'Can I use the phone in your room to tell Jacqueline now?'

'Of course,' my mum says.

After I've left the living room, I hear her say to my dad, 'I always said it wasn't healthy, being so much in someone else's pocket.'

'She's a loyal wee soul,' my dad replies. 'Maybe she felt she couldn't have other friends. Maybe she felt it would be abandoning Susan.'

Thirteen

'Do you know I've wondered that myself,' my mum says. 'I mean, I know the bullying could get nasty. I'd Janet Clarke here in tears about it more than once.'

'I'm proud of her, you know,' my dad says, 'sticking by Susan all those years.'

The skin all over my body is itching and burning. *It wasn't like that*, I want to shout. Neither of us cared about anything else. We used to do magic spells so that things people said would bounce right back at them. But then I think of Susan's final postcard. I don't want to hear any more. I tiptoe upstairs.

I walk over to Jacqueline's after lunch so we can spend the afternoon getting ready. I do her make-up and she does mine. It feels weird, being this close to her, her breath warm and damp, reeking of Juicy Fruit and cheese and onion Tayto, her fingers on my face. I can see the white-blonde hairs where she bleaches her moustache with Jolene, and I know she can see mine too.

'You've actually got quite big lips,' she says, as she strokes the bud of the lipgloss across them.

'Thanks,' I say, not knowing what to say.

'I didn't say it was a good thing.'

I can't think of anything to say to that.

'I'm only joking,' she says. 'Blot.'

I press my lips too hard against the square of toilet paper she holds out, smudging off too much lipgloss. When she rolls her eyes and goes to apply it again, I stop her.

'Wise up and don't be taking a pointy-head,' she says.

'I'm not,' I say.

'Didn't I say I was only joking? Big lips are good. BJ lips.' She looks at me sideways as she says it. She was one of the few I hadn't invited to my party; her and the Bible-bashers, who I knew wouldn't come. I've been waiting for weeks for her to bring it up. But she doesn't say any more, just layers on the gloopy pink lipgloss.

When our make-up's done, we get dressed. I'm wearing jeans and a lumberjack shirt, but Jacqueline says I should have worn a skirt. She opens her wardrobe, which is stuffed with clothes, hanging three or more to a hanger, bundled into cubbyholes, piled up in heaps. She picks out a skirt to lend me, a purple rah-rah from Kookaï. It's a bit crumpled but brand new, the tags still on. I wonder if she nicked it, or wants me to think she did. The girls in our class talk all the time about shoplifting, to impress the boys. Strawberry lip balm from The Body Shop or Take That keyrings from Athena; eyeshadow duos or at the very least handfuls of penny mix from Woolworths. You do it in pairs or groups of three or four, partly so there's someone to keep their eyes peeled for security guards but mostly so there's some-one to see you do it.

Jacqueline is watching for my reaction as I hold the skirt up against me. 'You can keep it if you want,' she says. She adds, quickly, 'I never really liked it anyway.'

'I don't know,' I say. 'It doesn't really go with my shirt.'

'Duh,' she says, and sniggers to an imaginary audience of Vicky Shaws and Alison Reids. She hokes through one of the cubbyholes and hands me a strappy vest top.

'I have loads of these,' she says. 'My dad buys me what-ever I want. He's so pathetic.' Then she says, 'What?'

'I didn't say anything.'

'Well, he is. He doesn't even look at the price tags. He's such a dickhead.'

'Yeah,' I say, vaguely.

'What do you mean, "yeah"? You haven't even met him. I'm only having you on. Keep that, too, if you want.'

I turn away to get undressed, but I can feel her watching me, feel her eyes, narrowed, sliding up my bare back. I yank on the vest top as quickly as possible and wriggle my jeans off only when I've put the skirt on over them.

When it's Jacqueline's turn to try on outfits, I pretend to be reading one of her *More!* magazines. 'Bet you're looking at Position of the Fortnight,' she says, 'you wee hallion.'

When we're both dressed, she makes us pose together in front of the mirror. 'Looking good, wee dolls,' she says, and puts her arm through mine. After a couple of seconds, I take my arm away. 'What?' she says. I pretend, too late, that I'm adjusting my ponytail. 'Everyone still says you and Susan Clarke were lesbos, you know,' she says. Then she says, before I can reply, 'Oh my God, I'm only joking. Can't you even take a joke?'

As we're leaving the house, she shouts to her mum that we're away out. Her mum, who's sat in front of the TV with a puffy face and unwashed hair, doesn't ask where we're going or when we'll be back. I think of the rumours that Jacqueline's dad pushed her mum right through the French doors, shattering them all over the patio and smashing her collarbone.

We walk up and down the high street for a while. We don't meet anyone we know, which I'm secretly glad about, because I don't want anyone to see me with Jacqueline Dunne. Then I feel mean for feeling that way. Janet Clarke always used to say, 'You have to give people a second chance, then another second chance, then a third second chance after that.' I push the thought of Janet Clarke from my head.

It starts to rain. We sit in the bus shelter and watch the old ladies in the doorway of the musty old tea room across the way, saying their goodbyes, wringing each other's hands, kissing each other's powdery dry cheeks with puckered lips, as the stout waitress stacks chairs on tables behind them. It's funny to think of old people having best friends. I try to say this to Jacqueline, but she pretends to mishear me and says, 'You like to think of old people having sex? That is so minging, you weirdo,' and cracks up at herself. The moment is gone then, and I don't try again. I'm not sure what I even meant in the first place. We sit there, not quite touching. The street lights come on. A queue starts to form outside the Silver Leaf. 'Why don't we share a gravy chip?' I say, without thinking.

Jacqueline looks at me like I'm mental. 'You have to have an empty stomach,' she says.

'Oh yeah,' I say, remembering too late. She means for the alcohol to work. You have to down it through a straw and on an empty stomach. Everyone knows that. She can't stop smirking, and I know that she's storing it up to tell the first person she can in Form Time on Monday. She's probably storing all of it up, everything I've done and said since I got to hers.

I could just walk off, I think. I could just walk all the way home. Except that my clothes and overnight things are at hers. Except that of course I can't.

'Are we just going to sit here all night or what?' I say.

'Pointy-head on you!' Jacqueline says. 'Fine, let's go.'

We cross the road to the Winemark and stand outside until a couple of students going in agree to buy us a carry-out. Jacqueline tells them we want a bottle of strawberry Ravers and hands over some money. I'm pretty sure by the careful way she pronounces *strawberry Ravers* that she's never done this before either, but neither of us is letting on to the other.

'Did you and Susan used to get blocked together?' she says, airily, as we turn into the side alley to wait. I don't want to admit that we never did, so I say, just as airily, 'Yeah.'

'What did you used to drink?' she says.

'Oh,' I say, and then it comes into my mind from nowhere, the drink my mum once ordered at the Knock Golf Club Christmas party: 'Pernod and blackcurrant, mostly,' I say, and Jacqueline goes quiet.

When the students hand over the bottle, we both stare at it for a moment. 'Give it here,' I say, as if I know what I'm doing, and I stick in my straw and manage nearly a quarter of the bottle. It doesn't taste as bad as I'd expected. It's a bit like the red marshmallow penny sweets from the very bottom of the tub in the newsagent's, sticky and slightly melted. Jacqueline has her go and passes it back to me. We've the whole bottle finished in less than five minutes.

'We're going to be blocked,' she says.

To my surprise, I giggle. I can feel the glow of it already, sweet and fuzzy and tingling, spreading from my stomach and inside my limbs.

'Oh my God,' she says. 'You're blocked already. Come on then. We don't want to waste it.' She links arms, and this time I don't take mine away.

We weave up the road together like a bad three-legged race. It's still mizzling, but even the rain feels less wet with the strawberry Ravers inside you. An old lady mutters at us as we pass her, something about a night like this and the pair of yous in your figures, and we start giggling and then start laughing and laugh the rest of the way.

When we get to Cairnburn Park there are a few groups there already, at the benches, in the kiddie playground. We stand at the fence by the playground, looking for people from our year. The only light is from the street lights on Cairnburn Road, running along the far side of the playground. I know Cairnburn Park: I walk past it every day on my way to school, and when we do cross-country in PE we run circuits around it. I try to remind myself of this. But even the trees look somehow different in the dark.

'The peelers raided the park two weeks ago,' Jacqueline says.

'I know,' I say.

'They lifted the under-age drinkers and took them down the station.'

'Yeah, I know.'

'What would your folks do, like?'

'I don't know,' I say. It gives me a queasy, painful, pleasurable feeling, thinking about what my parents would do if I was lifted by the peelers for under-age drinking; like pressing your tongue hard into the bloody space where a tooth has just fallen out. 'Ground me?' I say.

'Obviously, like,' she says, and rolls her eyes. 'Obviously they'd ground you. I mean what else.'

'They might not though,' I say.

When he was thirteen, my father got himself paralytic on home brew that he and some friends made and stored under the floor of the scout hut. Three of them carried him home and propped him up on the doorstep for my grandma to find, then rang the bell and legged it.

'Yeah, but, duh, it's different for girls,' Jacqueline says, when I tell her this. Then she says, 'My da would bate the shite out of me.'

I feel her looking at me, and I don't know what to say. I tell myself that everyone knows Jacqueline Dunne's the biggest liar there is. She probably started the rumour about her mum and the French windows herself, just for attention. I shiver. I can feel the Ravers wearing off. Jacqueline's still waiting for me to say something. 'Maybe we should head on, just,' I say.

'What d'you mean?' she says.

I try to say it in a way that lets her off the hook, if she really is scared of her dad. 'It doesn't look like there's much going on anyway.'

'Wise up,' she says. 'We're not going anywhere. I paid for the carry-out, remember? It's a total waste of it if we just leave now.' Then she says, 'Are you sure you've done this before?'

'What?' I say.

'I said, are you sure you've done this before? With Susan Clarke. Like you said.'

She is smirking, and I am suddenly raging. I'm raging at her. I'm raging at my parents. I haven't let myself think about Susan for weeks, but now I'm raging at her too. We'd promised we'd do everything together. We'd promised. I don't want to be getting drunk and seeing fellas with Jacqueline Dunne. I don't want to know about Jacqueline's dad. I don't want to be the one she confides in. I don't want to have to do everything with her, for the rest of the year, for the rest of school. I don't even like her. It isn't fair. It just isn't fair.

'Are you okay?' Jacqueline says.

'No,' I say. She's taken aback at that.

'Here, I'm sorry, like,' she says, after a moment or two. 'I didn't mean it.'

'I need another drink,' I say.

'We don't have any more drink.'

'Duh. I'm not stupid.'

She blinks at me. 'I didn't mean you were,' she says. 'I just meant . . . we could go back and get some more, if you want?'

'I'm not walking all the way back to the offy and back.'

'I'll go, if you want.'

I look at her, her big moony face and wide eyes, and I realise that she's scared. She's scared that she has gone too far, that I will just walk away. She's scared that she needs me more than I need her after all. The realisation makes me weirdly tired. This is my life, this moment, here, right now, on a rainy November Saturday night in Cairnburn Park with Jacqueline Dunne.

'I'll pay,' she says. 'I mean, I don't mind paying.'

'Let's just ask someone,' I say.

'What do you mean?'

There are three fellas standing nearby with a six-pack of tins. 'Come on,' I say, and set off towards them.

'Oh my God,' I hear Jacqueline saying. 'You can't just do that. What are you doing?'

But I've already decided that I'm going to take myself down. 'All right,' I say to them, and point at the six-pack. 'Can we have one?'

'Aye, but it'll cost yous, but,' the fella nearest says.

'How much?' I say.

'Don't be a dick,' another of the fellas says. 'Give the wee girls a tin.'

The fella with the six-pack yanks one free and hands it over.

'Thanks,' I say, and peel open the tab. I take a swig and almost retch. It's sharp and warm and rancid-tasting.

'Would you look at the hack of her,' I hear Jacqueline saying. 'She can't handle her drink. It's embarrassing.'

The fellas laugh.

I ignore them: take another gulp, then another.

'Leave me some,' Jacqueline says, getting into her stride. 'And I don't mean the last ten per cent. I don't want your slabbers.' The fellas laugh again, and the tallest one, who has black hair in curtains, says, 'What's your names?'

'I'm Brooke,' Jacqueline says, 'and my friend there's Winona.'

'Winona?' I say.

'Don't tell me you're too drunk already to know your own name,' she says.

'Winona?' the fella with curtains says. 'Like Winona Ryder?'

'My name's not Winona,' I say. 'I don't know why you're calling me Winona, Jacqueline.'

She glares at me.

'So your name's not Brooke either?' Curtains says.

'My middle name's Brooke,' Jacqueline says, shooting me another dirty look.

'You're mental, the both of yous,' Curtains says, but he and his friends are laughing, and another couple of tins are cracked open and passed around.

For the next few minutes, Jacqueline does most of the talking while I drink from my tin in steady gulps. She shares Curtains' tin, taking extravagant swigs and acting more and more blocked. I'm sure she's acting. I'm drinking my hardest and I don't feel anywhere near that yet.

When his tin runs out, Curtains opens his jacket and shows Jacqueline a quarter bottle of vodka. 'Will we go for a dander and have a wee swally?' he says.

Jacqueline stops laughing. 'I mean, the thing is,' she says, 'the thing is I'm not sure I should leave my friend.'

'Your friend's fine,' Curtains says. 'Aren't you? Winona there's fine. And she's got these fellas to keep her company, sure.'

'Yeah,' Jacqueline says, 'hang on a sec,' and she turns to me and pulls me a few paces away. 'Are you going to see one of them?' she says. I shrug. 'Seriously – are you? 'Cause if you're not—'

'Are yous fighting over me, wee girls?' Curtains calls over, and cracks up.

'He's a ride, isn't he?' Jacqueline says. 'Wouldn't you say he was a ride?'

'He's okay,' I say.

'You're just jealous,' she says. 'You're jealous 'cause it's me he's interested in.'

'Seriously?' I say. 'Do you actually think that?'

'Oh my God, you so are,' she says.

'I'm not jealous of you, Jacqueline,' I say. 'He's not my type.'

'What do you mean?'

'I mean, he's not the type of fella I go for.'

'You're just trying to put me off him.'

'If you want to see him, just go on and see him.' Then it occurs to me. 'Have you ever seen a wee lad before?'

'Course I have!' she says, too loud. 'And you're a fine one to talk. You hadn't seen anyone either before your party, and you let the lot of them do whatever they wanted to you. And in front of everyone. That's sick in the head. I think you're some sort of pervert. That's what everyone says, you know. You and that wee black bitch both.'

I stare at her. She flinches, as if I might be about to hit her. 'Are you not even going to say anything?' she says.

I say nothing.

'Here, are you coming or what?' Curtains shouts.

Jacqueline throws her shoulders back. 'Aye, sure,' she says, still looking at me.

'The funny thing is,' I say, as she takes a step backwards, 'she was just as white as she was black. No one ever took her mum into consideration.'

Jacqueline stares at me now. 'You are seriously weird,' she says. She turns and walks over to Curtains. He takes her hand, and they set off up the hill.

I go back to the dregs of my tin. I feel suddenly drunk, and it's not a nice feeling. The cider is a sloshy mass in my tummy that might surge upwards at any moment, and the vision in my left eye is blurring. My heart is pounding, pounding and pounding, as if I've just run circuits around the park. I lean against the wooden frame of the kiddie castle and try to concentrate on breathing.

The two remaining fellas exchange a few words, and the spotty one slopes off. The other one moves in to stand beside me. His hair is gelled into a crispy comb across his forehead, and one of his ears is pierced with a small gold ring. He's wearing a Coq Sportif jacket. I can't think of a single thing to say to him. We stand side by side and pass his tin back and forth. I don't want any more to drink. I plug the hole with my tongue and pretend to swallow. From time to time he asks a question: 'So you come here most weekends then', 'So are you blocked yet?' Sometimes he asks the same question a few minutes later. He is drunk, I realise – even drunker than me.

'Here,' he eventually slurs, 'so are you going to see us or what?'

I glance around, but Jacqueline is nowhere to be seen.

Coq Sportif leans in closer. 'Are you?' he says. His breath is sharp with cider and thick with cigarettes. His lips are thin and flaking. They skim my earlobe. 'Come on.'

It's your own fault, I tell myself. *You've only got yourself to blame.* I close my eyes for a second then nod.

'You are, aye?' he says.

'I am, aye,' I say.

'Come on then,' he says, and makes a grab for my hand. His hand is damp, and I can feel what I think is a wart on the pad of his thumb, but I don't know how to make him let go. We walk up the hill and down the path a bit, passing other couples. None of them is Jacqueline and Curtains.

'In here,' Coq Sportif says, and we wriggle through some trampled scratchy bushes to a tree stump.

'Right,' Coq Sportif says, and we sit down. Almost immediately he leans in to kiss me, but he leans too forcefully and our teeth clash. He pulls away. 'Jeez, take it easy,' he says, and laughs to himself. Then he dives in again. It seems to go on for ever, and I wonder if I can break it off without being rude. But I'm more worried that if I move too suddenly I'll throw up.

Eventually he pulls away, and I shift sideways. The tree stump is cold under my bare thighs, and water is dripping from the branches above onto my shoulders and neck. I can feel my body breaking out into gooseflesh, all over, arms and legs and even places like my stomach.

'All right?' he says.

'Yeah,' I say.

'Dead on.'

For a moment I think that it's over. But he comes at me again, this time shoving a hand up my skirt as well. I freeze. I feel him plucking at the elastic of my knickers. All I can think about is the wart on his thumb. I feel the cider swirling at the base of my throat. He breaks off the kissing and says something.

'Sorry?' I whisper, and he slurs it again. Then, without waiting for an answer, he hoiks my skirt up around my waist and tugs my knickers to one side and pushes a finger inside of me. I can't seem to move. I try to concentrate on the sound of raindrops falling from the branches around and above us, on the sound of the little stream. I try to imagine myself dissolving, washing away in drops into the earth and the water.

Coq Sportif is wiggling his finger. Then he stops. He pulls his hand away and shakes it out.

'Oh my God,' I say.

'What is it?'

I lurch to my feet, and the cider spews from me in a hot watery gush. Almost as soon as it's happened I feel better.

'What the fuck?' Coq Sportif is saying. 'Did you just boke?'

I straighten my clothes and take a couple of exploratory steps. My legs are weak and fuzzy, but they hold me up.

'Actually,' I say, 'I'd better be going. My friend will be waiting.'

'Ach, wise up,' he says, 'for fuck's sake, like,' but when I move away he doesn't stop me.

I find Jacqueline by the slide getting off with some fella who isn't Curtains. She's completely stocious. I walk right up to them and pull her away by the shoulder. 'Jacqueline,' I say, 'we have to go now.'

'What are you at?' the fella says.

'Look at the state of her,' I say. 'We've got to go.'

'Fuck away off, then,' the fella says, and staggers backwards against the slide.

'Come on, Jacqueline,' I say, and I take her by the elbow and put my other arm around her. I manage to get her over the stile, and then she staggers to the side of the car park to be sick. She's sick once, and then again, and then a third time. I think, *I should hold her hair back*. It takes a moment or two before I can make myself, but then I walk up to her and gather it all back into a bundle. She's crying, huge snotty tears, and moaning in incoherent gulps. With my spare hand I pat her shoulder. 'It's going to be okay,' I tell her. I don't mean it, but I say it, over and over: 'It's going to be okay.' It occurs to me that she's made it easier, by saying what she said. I'd already decided that after tonight I wasn't going to be friends with Jacqueline Dunne any more.

After she's finished chucking up, we set off back to hers. She's so weak it takes us almost an hour to get there, a walk that should be fifteen minutes at most. When we finally make it, I get her keys from her pocket and let us in. There's no sign of Mrs Dunne, or Mr Dunne.

I steer Jacqueline up the stairs and into her room as quietly as I can, and onto her bed. Her jacket is covered in vomit, and I manage to get it off her, pushing and tugging one arm at a time. Her vest top and skirt are spattered with vomit too, but I can't risk it getting round that I took them off her. So I just pull off her boots and tuck her duvet round her.

Then I tiptoe to the bathroom and pee, wash the stupid make-up off and brush my teeth for several minutes, trying to scrape the feel and taste of Coq Sportif away. Back in Jacqueline's room I get into my pyjamas and wriggle down into my sleeping bag. Then I close my eyes and try to ignore how hard the floor is under the thin carpet, try to think myself elsewhere, anywhere but here.

I think myself back into the Clarkes' house, before they've left for London; into their living room. It's the Saturday before they leave, and their boxes and crates have been shipped to London, and their furniture has been put into storage until they find somewhere permanent to live. The living room is strange and echoey without anything in it. We are lying there, me and Susan and Michael, like we used to do when we were children and the three of us would have midnight feasts. We've stayed up talking until it's getting light again outside and Susan can't stay awake any longer. Her eyes keep closing then jerking open before slowly closing again, and eventually she is asleep.

'Are you still awake?' Michael says after a while. He is lying beside the empty fireplace, and Susan and I are over beside where the red sofa used to be, with me in the middle.

'Yes,' I say, rolling onto my tummy. 'Are you?' and I hear him laugh softly.

'No,' he says.

'Shut up,' I say and reach over to play-punch his arm. He grabs my wrist and holds it, and holds it a moment longer than he should have. My tummy flips. 'Are you going to give me my hand back?' I say, when I can speak again.

'No,' he says, but he lets go. I flex my wrist. My wrist, my whole arm, seems to be tingling.

'Here, I didn't hurt you, did I?' he says, after a minute.

'I think you might have done,' I say. 'I think you might actually have broken it.' It is the way we've always talked to each other: a teasing, easy kind of banter, as if I'm another sister.

But he doesn't smile or roll his eyes like he usually does. 'Tell me,' he says. 'Tell me if this is—'

And then he leans forward and kisses me.

'Pastie-lip,' people used to call him, to call him and Susan both. But his lips are pillowy and soft, softer than I've ever imagined a boy's lips can be, and the kiss is perfect, a long, slow pull of a kiss.

Afterwards, he inches his sleeping bag even closer to mine, and we lie there holding hands for what seems like hours.

Jacqueline moans in her sleep, and the spell is broken. My mouth is dry and furry and my head is starting to thump. I need a drink of water. I unzip my sleeping bag and get to my feet as carefully as I can. Even though I'm moving slowly, I have a massive head rush and have to grab onto the bed knob to support myself. Jacqueline twists to one side and then the other, whimpering. I should bring her a glass of water, too, I think.

I tiptoe to the bathroom, feeling my way along the upper landing. I take the toothbrushes out of their ceramic mug and fill up that. I drink down two mugfuls, three, and nothing has ever tasted so good. I fill up the mug again to bring back to the bedroom.

I lift up Jacqueline's head and manage to get a few sips of water into her, though most of it dribbles down her chin. I realise that I'm imagining that Janet Clarke is here, watching what a Good Samaritan I am.

A memory comes: a time Janet asked us to help her carry the Easter flowers to church. Susan and Michael grumbled, and I pretended to as well, but inside I loved it: we were like a procession, Janet at the front with the tall stems of catkins and pussy willow she'd cut from the trees in their garden, us following behind with the bundles of Queen Anne's lace and the calla lilies. I was walking beside her, and she sang the whole way, tunes whose words were about other worlds and other places, love and sacrifice and soldiering on. When people in the street turned to look at us, you saw they were assuming that I was her real daughter. I was used to that, though it was something that Susan and I never, ever spoke about.

But that morning it gave me a hot, secret, glad feeling.

The Clarkes are gone, I tell myself. I make myself say it out loud: 'The Clarkes are gone.' It comes out more forcefully than I'd intended, and Jacqueline opens her eyes. They are glassy and unfocused, and I wonder if I should wake her mum, despite the trouble Jacqueline might be in with her dad. Then I see her recognise me, and she opens her mouth and tries to speak. 'You're okay,' I tell her. 'You're back home in your own bed. See if you can drink a wee bit more of this.' I tilt the mug towards her lips. She gulps, swallows. 'I'll leave the rest of it here,' I say, and set it on her bedside table, where she can reach it.

Then I wriggle back down into my sleeping bag and turn on my side to wait for morning to come. It will come, I tell myself. It will, it will, it has to, and one day all of this will be long ago, as if it happened in another place, another time, and maybe I won't ever think about it any more, and even if I do, it'll already be over.

Poison

I SAW HIM LAST NIGHT. He was with a girl half his age, more than half, a third of his age. It was in the bar of the Merchant Hotel, and they were together on the raspberry crushed-velvet banquette. Her arm was flung around his shoulder, and he had an arm around her, too, an easy hand on her waist. She was laughing, her face turned right up to his, enthralled, delighted. They kept clinking glasses: practically every time they took a sip of their cocktails they clinked glasses. I was alone, in a high seat at the bar, waiting for my friends – friends I hadn't seen in years but who, even years ago, were always late. I'd ordered a glass of white wine while I waited; I picked it up with shaking hands. It was him. There was no doubt about it. His face had got pouchy, and his hair, though still black – dyed, surely – was limp and thinning. When he stood up, he was shorter than I remembered.

But it was him.

I hadn't seen him in years. I scrambled to work out the numbers in my head. Sixteen – seventeen – almost eight-een. All those years later, and there he was, entwined with a girl a fraction of his age. He must be nearly sixty now.

Poison

I bent my head over the cocktail list as he walked towards me, letting my hair fall partly over my face, but I couldn't take my eyes off him. His eyes slid over the women he passed, thin, fake-tanned bare backs and sequinned dresses, stripper shoes. He didn't look once at me. I'd lived away too long, and I'd forgotten how dressed up people got for a Saturday night: I was in skinny jeans and a blazer, and not enough make-up. I watched him walk along the candy-striped carpet and out towards the toilets, and then I turned to look at his companion.

She had her head bowed over her phone, and she was jiggling one leg and rapidly texting. She suddenly looked very young indeed. I'd put her in her mid-twenties, but it was less than that. I felt a strange tightness in my chest. She put her phone away and uncrossed her legs, recrossed them, tugged at the hem of her little black dress. She picked up her empty glass and tilted her head right back and drained the dregs, coughed a little, set the glass back down and slung her hair over the other shoulder. She had too much make-up on: huge swipes of blusher, exaggerated cat-eyes. She glanced around the bar, then she took out her phone again, flicked and tapped at it. She wasn't used to being alone in a bar like this. It was an older crowd and she felt self-conscious, you could tell. The men in the chairs opposite her were in their forties at least, heavy-jowled, sweating in their suits, tipping back their whiskey sours. I watched the relief on her face when he appeared again, how she wriggled into him and kissed him on the cheek. As they studied the menu together, giggling, their heads bent confidentially together, I suddenly realised she wasn't his lover.

She was his daughter.

She was Melissa. Seventeen years. She'd be eighteen now. Perhaps they were out tonight celebrating her eighteenth birthday. With a surge of nausea I realised, then, that what I'd been feeling wasn't outrage that she was too young for him, or contempt, or disgust. It was simpler, and much more complicated than that.

★

I don't remember whose idea it was to go to Mr Knox's house. One minute we were giggling over him, nudging elbows and sugar-breath and damp heads bent together, and the next minute someone was saying they knew where he lived, something about a neighbour and church and his wife, and suddenly, almost without the decision being made, it was decided we were going there.

Was it Tanya?

There were four of us: Donna, Tanya, Lisa and me. We were fourteen, and bored. It was a Baker day, which meant no school, and we had nothing else to do. It was April, and chilly, rain coming in gusty, intermittent bursts. The Easter holidays had only just ended, and none of us had any pocket money left. We'd met in Cairnburn Park just after nine, but at that time on a wet Monday morning it was deserted. We'd wandered down to the kiddie playground, but the swings were soaking, and, after a half-hearted couple of turns on the roundabout, we'd given up. The four of us had trailed down Sydenham Avenue and past our school — it was strange to see the lights on in the main building and the teachers' cars all lined up as usual.

Then, more out of habit than anything else, we crossed the road to the Mini-Market. We pooled our spare change to buy packets of strawberry bon-bons and Midget Gems, and Donna nicked a handful of fizzy cola bottles. We ate them as we trudged on down towards Ballyhackamore. The rain was getting heavier, and none of us had umbrellas, so we ended up in KFC, huddled over the melamine table, slurping a shared Pepsi.

We were the only ones in there. The sugar and the rain and the boredom made us restless, and snide. We'd started telling a story, in deliberately too-loud voices, about someone who'd ordered a plain chicken burger and complained when it came with mayo. There's no mayo in it, the person behind the counter had said. Oh yes there is. Oh no there isn't. And it turned out that the mayo was actually a burst sac of pus from a cyst growing on the chicken breast.

The girl behind the counter was giving us increasingly dirty looks, and we realised that if she chucked us out we really had nowhere to go, so we changed tack then and started slagging each other, boys we'd fancied, boys we'd seen or wanted to see.

And then the conversation, almost inevitably, turned to Mr Knox.

We all fancied Mr Knox. No one even bothered to deny it. The whole school fancied him. He was the French and Spanish teacher, and he was part French himself, or so the rumours went. He was part something, anyway: he had to be – he was so different from the other teachers. He had dark hair that he wore long and floppy over one eye and permanent morning-after stubble, and he smoked Camel cigarettes. Teachers couldn't smoke anywhere in the school grounds, not even in the staffroom, but he smoked anyway, in the staff toilets in the Art Block or in the caretakers' shed, girls said, and if you had him immediately after break or lunch you smelt it off him. He drove an Alfa Romeo, bright red, and where the other male teachers were rumpled in browns and greys, he wore coloured silk shirts and loafers. On Own Clothes Day at the end of term he'd worn tapered jeans and a polo neck and Chelsea boots and, even though it was winter, mirrored aviator sunglasses, like an off-duty film star. He had posters on his classroom walls of Emmanuelle Béart and a young Catherine Deneuve and Soledad Miranda, and he lent his sixth-formers videos of Pedro Almodóvar films.

But that wasn't all. A large part of his charge came from the fact that he'd had an affair with a former pupil, Davina Calvert. It had been eight years ago, and they were married now. He'd left his wife for her, and it was a real scandal. He'd almost lost his job over it, except in the end they couldn't dismiss him because he'd done nothing strictly, legally wrong.

It had happened before we joined the school, but we knew all the details: everyone did. It was almost a rite of passage to cluster as first- or second-years in a corner of the library poring over old school magazines in search of her, hunting down grainy black-and-white photographs of year groups, foreign exchange trips, prize days, tracking her as she grew up to become his lover.

Davina Calvert, Davina Knox. She was as near and as far from our lives as it was possible to get.

Davina, the story went, was her year's star pupil. She got the top mark in Spanish A Level in the whole of Northern Ireland and came third in French. Davina Calvert, Davina Knox. Nothing happened between them while she was still at school – or nothing anyone could pin on him, at least – but when she left she went on a gap year, teaching English in Granada, and he went out to visit her. We knew this for sure because Lisa's older sister had been two years below Davina Calvert and was in Mr Knox's Spanish A-Level class at the time. After Hallowe'en half-term, he turned up with a load of current Spanish magazines, *Hola!* and *Diez Minutos* and Spanish *Vogue*. They asked him if he'd been away, and where he'd been, and he answered them in a teasing torrent of Spanish that none of them could quite follow. But it went around the school like wildfire that he'd been in Granada, visiting Davina Calvert, and, sure enough, when she was back for Christmas, at least two people saw them in his Alfa Romeo, parked up a side street, kissing, and by the end of the school year he and his wife were separated, getting divorced.

The following year, he didn't even pretend to hide it from his classes: when they talked about what they'd done at the weekend, he'd grin and say, in French or Spanish, that he'd been visiting a special friend in Edinburgh. Everyone knew it was Davina.

We used to picture what it must have been like, when he first visited her in Granada. The winding streets and white medieval buildings. The blue and orange and purple sky. They would have walked together to Lorca's house and the Alhambra, and, afterwards, clinked glasses of sherry in some cobbled square with fountains and Gypsy musicians. Perhaps he would have reached under the table to stroke her thigh, slipping a hand under her skirt and tracing the curve of it up, and, when he withdrew it, she would have crossed and uncrossed her legs, squeezing and releasing her thighs, the tingling pressure unbearable.

I imagined it countless times, but I could never quite settle on what would have happened next. What would you do, in Granada, with Mr Knox? Would you lead him back to your little rented room, in the sweltering eaves of a homestay or a shared apartment? No: you'd go with him instead to the hotel that he'd booked, a sumptuous four-poster bed in a grand and faded parador in the Albayzín – or more likely an anonymous room in the new district where the staff wouldn't ask questions, a room where the bed had white sheets with clinical corners, a room with a bathroom you could hear every noise from. The shame of it – the excitement.

And in the KFC on the Upper Newtownards Road, on that rainy Monday Baker day in April, we knew where Mr Knox and Davina lived. It was out towards the Ice Bowl, near the golf club, in Dundonald. It was a forty-, forty-five-minute walk. We had nothing else to do. We linked arms and set off.

It was an anticlimax when we got there. We'd walked down the King's Road, passing such posh houses on the way; somehow, with the sports car and the sunglasses and the designer suits, we'd expected his house to be special too. But most of the houses on his street were just like ours: bungalows, or small red-brick semis, with hedges and lawns and rhododendron bushes. We walked up one side and down the other. There was nothing to tell us where he lived: no sign of him.

We were starting to bicker by then. The rain was coming down relentless, and Tanya was getting worried that someone might see us and report us to the school. We slagged her – how would anyone know we were doing anything wrong, and how would they know which school we went to anyway, we weren't in uniform – but all of us were slightly on edge. It was only mid-morning, but what if he left school for some reason, or came home for an early lunch? All four of us were in his French class, and me and Lisa had him for Spanish too: he'd recognise us.

We should go: we knew we should go. The long walk back in the rain stretched ahead of us. We sat on a low wall to empty our pockets and purses and work out if we had enough to pay for a bus ticket each. When it turned out there was only enough for three, we started squabbling: Tanya had no money left, but she'd paid for the bon-bons, and almost half of the Pepsi, so it wasn't fair if she had to walk. Well, it wasn't fair for everyone to have to walk just because of her. Besides, she lived nearest: there was least distance for her to walk. But it wasn't fair! Back and forth it went, and it might have turned nasty – Donna had just threatened to slap Tanya if she didn't quit whingeing.

Then we saw Davina.

It was Lisa who recognised her, at the wheel of a metallic-blue Peugeot. The car swept past us and round the curve of the road, but Lisa swore it had been her at the wheel. We leapt up, galvanised, and looked at each other. 'Well, come on,' Donna said.

'Donna!' Tanya said.

'What, are you scared?' Donna said. Donna had thick glasses that made her eyes look small and mean, and she'd pushed her sister through a patio door in a fight. We were all a little scared of Donna.

'Come on,' Lisa said.

Tanya looked as if she was about to cry.

'We're just going to look,' I said. 'We're just going to walk past and look at the house. There's no law against that.' Then I added, 'For fuck's sake, Tanya.' I didn't mind Tanya, if it was just the two of us, but it didn't do to be too friendly with her in front of the others.

'Yeah, Tanya, for fuck's sake,' Lisa said.

Tanya sat back down on the wall. 'I'm not going anywhere,' she said. 'We'll be in such big trouble.'

'Fine,' Donna said. 'Fuck off home, what are you waiting for?' She turned and linked Lisa's arm, and they started walking down the street.

'Come on, Tan,' I said.

'I have a bad feeling,' she said. 'I just don't think we should.' But when I turned to go after the others, she pushed herself from the wall and followed.

We found the house where the Peugeot was parked, right at the bottom of the street. It was the left-hand side of a semi, and it had an unkempt hedge and a stunted palm tree in the middle of the little front lawn. You somehow didn't picture Mr Knox with a miniature palm tree in his garden. We clustered on the opposite side of the road, half hidden behind a white van, giggling at it. And then we realised that Davina was still in the car. 'What's she at?' Donna said. 'Stupid bitch.'

We stood and watched a while longer, but nothing happened. You could see the dark blur of her head and the back of her shoulders, just sitting there.

'Well, fuck this for a game of soldiers,' Donna said. 'I'm not standing here all day like a big fucking lemon.' She turned and walked a few steps down the road and waited for the rest of us to follow.

'Yeah,' Tanya said. 'I'm going too. I said I'd be home for lunch.'

Neither Lisa nor I moved.

'What do you think she's doing?' Lisa said.

'Listening to the radio?' I said. 'Mum does that, sometimes, if it's *The Archers*. She doesn't want to leave the car until it's over.'

'I suppose,' Lisa said, looking disappointed.

'Come on,' Tanya said. 'We've seen where he lives, now let's just go.'

47

Donna was standing with her hands on her hips, annoyed that we were ignoring her. 'Seriously,' she shouted. 'I'm away on.'

They were expecting me and Lisa to follow, but we didn't. As soon as they were out of earshot, Lisa said, 'God, Donna's doing my fucking head in today.' She glanced at me sideways as she said it.

'Hah,' I said, vaguely. It didn't do to be too committal: Lisa and Donna were thick as thieves these days. Lisa's mum and mine had gone to school together, and the two of us had been friends since we were babies. There were photographs of us in the bath together, covered in bubbles, bashing each other with bottles of Mr Matey. We'd been inseparable through primary school, and into secondary. Recently though Lisa had started hanging out more with Donna, smoking Silk Cuts nicked from Donna's mum and drinking White Lightning in the park at weekends. Both of them had gone pretty far with boys. Not full-on sex, but close, or so they both claimed. I'd kissed a boy once. It was better than Tanya – but still; it made me weird and awkward around Lisa when it was just the two of us. I'd always imagined we'd do everything together, like we always had done.

I could feel Lisa still looking at me. I scuffed the ground with the heel of one of my gutties.

'I mean, seriously doing my head in,' she said, and she pulled a face that was recognisably an impression of Donna, and I let myself start giggling. Lisa looked pleased. 'Here,' she said, and she slipped her arm through mine. 'What do you think Davina's like? I mean, d'you know what I mean?'

I knew exactly what she meant. 'Well, she's got to be gorgeous,' I said.

'You big lesbo,' Lisa said, digging me in the ribs.

I dug her back. 'No, being serious. She's got to be: he left his wife for her. She's got to be gorgeous.'

'What else?'

'Well, she doesn't care what people think. I mean, think of all the gossip. Think of what you'd say to your parents and that.'

'My dad would go nuts.'

'Yeah,' I said.

We were silent for a moment then, watching the blurred figure in the Peugeot.

'D'you think anything did happen while they were at school?' Lisa suddenly said. 'I mean, it must have, mustn't it? Otherwise why would you bother going all that way to visit her? I mean, like, lying to your wife and flying all the way to Granada.'

'I know. I don't know.'

I'd wondered about it before — we all had. But it was especially strange, standing right outside his house, his and Davina's. Did she linger at his desk after class? Did he stop and give her a lift somewhere? Did she hang around where he lived and bump into him, as if by chance, or pretend she was having problems with her Spanish grammar? Who started it? And how exactly did it start? And did either of them ever imagine it would end up here?

'She might have been our age,' Lisa said.

'I know.'

'Or only, like, two or three years older.'

'I know.'

We must have been standing there for ten minutes by now. A minute longer and we might have turned to go. But all of a sudden the door of the Peugeot swung open, and Davina got out. There she was: Davina Calvert, Davina Knox.

Except that the Davina in our heads had been glamorous, like the movie sirens on Mr Knox's classroom walls, but this Davina had messy hair in a ponytail and dark circles under her eyes, and she was wearing baggy jeans and a raincoat. And she was crying: her face was puffy, and she was crying, openly, tears just running down her face.

I felt Lisa take my hand and squeeze it. 'Oh my God,' she breathed.

We watched Davina walk around to the other side of the car and unstrap a toddler from the back seat. She lifted him to his feet and then hauled a baby car seat out.

We had forgotten – if we'd ever known – that Mr Knox had babies. He never mentioned them, or had photos on his desk like some of the other teachers. You somehow didn't think of Mr Knox with babies.

'Oh my God,' Lisa said again.

The toddler was wailing. We watched Davina wrestle him up the drive and into the porch, the car seat over the crook of her other arm. She had to put it down while she found her keys, and we watched as she scrabbled in her bag and then her coat pockets before locating them, unlocking the door and going inside. The door swung shut behind her.

We stood there for a moment longer. Then, 'Come on,' I found myself saying. 'Let's knock on her door.' I have no idea where the impulse came from, but as soon as I said it I knew I was going to do it.

Lisa turned to face me. 'Are you insane?'

'Come on,' I said.

'But what will we say?'

'We'll say we're lost, we'll say we're after a glass of water – I don't know. We'll think of something. Come on.'

Lisa stared at me. 'Oh my God, you're mad,' she said. But she giggled. And then we were crossing the road and walking up the driveway, and there we were, standing in Mr Knox's porch. 'You're not seriously going to do this?' Lisa said.

'Watch me,' I said, and I fisted my hand and knocked on the door.

I can still picture every moment of what happens next.

Davina opens the door (Davina Calvert, Davina Knox) with the baby in one arm and the toddler hanging off one of her legs. We blurt out – it comes to me, inspired – that we live just round the corner, and we're going door to door to see does anyone need a babysitter. All at once, we're like a team again, me and Leese. I start a sentence, she finishes it. She says something, I elaborate. We sound calm, and totally plausible. Davina says thank you, but the baby's too young to be left. Lisa says can we leave our details anyway, for maybe in a few months' time? Davina blinks and says okay, sure, and the two of us inch our way into her hallway while she gets a pen and notelet from the phone pad. Lisa calls me Judith, and I call her Carol. We write down Judith and Carol and give a made-up number. We are invincible. We are on fire. Davina says what school do we go to, and Lisa says, not missing a beat, Dundonald High. Why aren't you at school today, Davina asks, and I say it's a Baker day. I suddenly wonder if all schools have the same Baker days, and a dart of fear goes through me, but Davina just says, Oh, and doesn't ask anything more.

We sense she's going to usher us out now, and before she can do it, Lisa asks what the baby's called, and Davina says, Melissa. That's a pretty name, I say, and Davina says thank you. So we admire the baby, her screwed-up little face and flexing fingers, and I think of having Mr Knox's baby growing inside you, and a huge rush of heat goes through me. When Davina says, as we knew she was going to, Girls, as I'm sure you can see, I've really got my hands full here, and Lisa says, No, no, of course, we'll have to be going – and she's getting the giggles now, I can see them rising in her, the way the corners of her lips pucker and tweak – I say, Yes, of course, but do you mind if I use your toilet first? Davina blinks again, her red-raw eyes, as if she can sense a trap but doesn't know quite what it is, and then she says no problem, but the downstairs loo's blocked, wee Reuben has a habit of flushing things down it, and they haven't got round to calling out the plumber, I'll have to go upstairs. It's straight up the stairs and first on the left. I can feel Lisa staring at me, but I don't meet her eye, I just say, Thank you, and make my way upstairs.

The bathroom is full – just humming – with Mr Knox. There's his dressing gown hung on the back of the door, his electric razor on the side of the sink, his can of Lynx deodorant on the window sill. There's his toothbrush in a mug, and there's flecks of his stubble in the sink, and there's his dirty clothes in the laundry basket. I kneel and open it and recognise one of his shirts, a slippery pale-blue one with yellow diamond patterning. I reach over and flush the toilet so the noise will cover my movements, and then I open the mirrored cabinet above the sink and run my fingers over the bottles on what must be his shelf, the shaving cream, the brown plastic bottle of prescription drugs, a six-pack of Durex condoms, two of them missing.

The skin all over my body is tingling, tingling in places I didn't know could tingle, in between my fingers, the backs of my knees. I ease one of the condoms from the strip, tugging gently along the foil perforations, and stuff it into my jeans. Then I put the box back, exactly as it was, and close the mirrored cabinet.

I stare at myself in the mirror. My face looks flushed. I wonder, again, what age she was when he first noticed her. I realise that I don't know how long I've been in here. I run the tap, and look around me one last time. And then, without planning to, without knowing I'm going to until I've done it, I find my hand closing around one of the bottles of perfume on the window sill and rearranging the others so the gap doesn't show. You're not supposed to keep perfume on the window sill anyway – even I know that. I slide it into the inside pocket of my jacket and arrange my left arm over it so the bulge doesn't show, then I turn off the tap and go downstairs to where Lisa's shooting me desperate glances.

Outside, she can't believe what I've done. None of them can. We catch up with Donna and Tanya still waiting for us on the main road. Although it feels like a lifetime has passed, it's only been ten minutes or so since they left us.

'You'll never believe what she did,' Lisa says, and there's pride in her voice as she tells them how we knocked on the door and went inside, inside Mr Knox's house, and talked to Davina, and touched the baby, and how I used his bathroom. I take over the story then. The condom I keep quiet about – that's mine, just for me – but I show them the perfume. It's a dark glass bottle, three-quarters full, aubergine, almost black, with a round glass stopper. In delicate gold lettering, it says, 'POISON, Dior'.

'I can't believe you nicked her fucking perfume!' Donna says.

Tanya stares at me as if she's going to be sick.

Donna takes the bottle from me and uncaps the lid. She aims it at Lisa.

'Fuck off,' Lisa says. 'You're not spraying that shit on me.'

'Spray me then,' I say, and they all look at me. 'Go on,' I say, 'spray me.' I roll up the sleeve of my jumper to bare my wrist.

Donna aims the nozzle. A jet of perfume shoots out, dark and heady and forbidden-smelling.

'Eww,' says Tanya, 'that smells like fox. Why would any-one want to smell like that?'

I press my wrists together carefully and raise them to my neck, dab both sides. It's the strongest perfume I've ever smelt. The musty green scent makes me feel slightly nauseous. It doesn't smell like a perfume you'd imagine Davina Calvert choosing: he must have bought it for her; it must be him that likes it. I wonder if he sprays it on her before they go out, if she holds up her wrists and bares her throat for him.

'What are you going to do with it?' Lisa says.

'We could bring it into school,' I say, and all at once my heart is racing again. 'We could bring it into school and spray it in his lesson. We could see what he does.'

'You're a fucking psycho,' Donna says, and she laughs, but for the first time ever it's tinged with awe.

'You can't,' Tanya's saying, 'I'm not having anything to do with this,' but we're all ignoring her now.

'Me and Lisa have Spanish tomorrow,' I say, 'straight after lunch. We'll do it then. Right, Leese?'

'What do you think he'll do?' Lisa says, wide-eyed.

'Maybe,' I say, 'he'll keep us behind after class and shag our brains out on his desk.' I say it as if I'm joking, and she and Donna laugh, and I laugh too, but I think of the condom hidden in my pocket and the tingling feeling returns.

That night, I lie in bed and squeeze my eyes closed and play the scene of them meeting in Granada with more intensity than ever before, and when I get to the part where he undoes her halter-neck top and eases her skirt off and lies her down on the bed, my whole body starts shaking.

The next day in Spanish, we did it, just as we'd planned. Before class started, we huddled over my bag and sprayed the Poison, unknotting our ties to mist it in the hollow of our throats. We were feverish with excitement.

He didn't know how close to him we'd got.

I had his condom with me too. I'd slept with it under my pillow, and now it was zipped into the pocket of my school skirt. I could feel the foil edge rubbing against my thigh when I crossed my legs.

Mr Knox came in, sat on the edge of his desk and asked us what we'd been doing over the weekend.

My heart was thumping. I suddenly wished I'd prepared something clever to say, something that would get his attention, or make him smile, but I hadn't, and I found myself saying the first thing that came into my head, just to be the one that spoke.

'Voy de compras,' I said.

'I'm sure you go shopping all the time, but in this instance it was in the past tense.' He looked straight at me as he said it, his crinkled eyes, a teasing smile. He seemed surprised, or amused, to see me talking. I was never one of the confident ones who spoke up in class without prompting. 'Otra vez, Señorita.'

Señorita. I'd never been one of the girls he called *señorita* before. I imagined he'd called Davina *señorita*. His accent in Spanish was rolling and sexy. Hers would be too, of course. They'd probably had conversations of their own, over and above everyone else's heads.

'Fui de compras,' I said, locking eyes with him.

'Muy bien, fuiste de compras, y qué compraste?'

'What did I buy?' The cloying smell of the perfume was making me dizzy, and I couldn't seem to straighten my thoughts.

'Si – qué compraste?'

'Compré – compré un nuevo perfume.'

'Muy bien.' He grinned at me. 'Fuiste de compras, y compraste un nuevo perfume. Muy bien.'

'Do you want to smell it, Mr Knox?' Lisa blurted.

'Lisa!' I hissed, delighted and appalled.

'Gracias, Lisa, pero no.'

'Are you sure? I think you'd like it.'

'Gracias, Lisa. Who's next?' He gazed around the room, waiting for someone else to put their hand up. I'd said it: I couldn't believe I'd said it. I felt the colour rising to my face. Lisa was stifling a fit of giggles beside me, but I ignored her and kept my eyes on Mr Knox. He hadn't flinched.

At the end of class, we hung about, taking our time to pack our bags and wondering if he'd keep us behind, but he didn't. We left the room and fell into each other's arms in fits of giggles, but we were exaggerating, both of us kidding ourselves that we weren't disappointed. Or at least I was. Maybe for Lisa it was just a big joke. I don't know what I'd expected, exactly, but I'd expected something – a moment of recognition, something.

My last lesson of the day was Maths, where I sat with Tanya – none of our other friends were taking Higher Maths. We walked out of school together. Tanya lived up by Stormont, and it was out of my way, but I sometimes walked home with her anyway. My mum had gone back to work since my dad moved out, and I didn't like going back to an empty house. And today there was the increased attraction of knowing that this was the way Mr Knox must drive home.

We walked down Wandsworth and crossed the busy junction, then up the Upper Newtownards Road. When we got to the traffic lights at Castlehill Road, by Stormont Presbyterian, I kept us hanging about. I made sure I was standing facing the traffic. I was waiting for the Alfa Romeo to pass us. I knew in my bones that it would, knew that it had to. When it did, I turned to watch it and didn't take my eyes from it until it was gone completely from sight. And by the time I turned back, something inside me had shifted.

I spent an hour that night learning extra French vocab and practising my Spanish tenses, determined to impress him the following day, to make him notice me. The next day, I walked home with Tanya again, and the day after that, and pretty soon I was walking home with her every day. It was a twenty-minute walk from school to hers, and most days by the time we reached the Upper Newtownards Road his car would be long gone. But I took to noting which days he held his after-school language club for sixth-formers, or had staff meetings, and on those days I'd try to time our journey, persuading Tanya to come to the Mini-Market with me and killing time there choosing sweets and looking at the magazines, then lingering at the traffic lights by the church in the hope of seeing his car.

On the days that I did, even just a flash of it as it sped past through a green light, I'd feel I was flying all the way home.

Lisa and Donna were friends again, and Lisa still didn't invite me on their Cairnburn nights, but suddenly I didn't care. Three Saturday evenings in a row I let my mum think I was going to Lisa's, and I walked the whole way to Mr Knox and Davina's house, and I walked past two, three, four, five times and saw both cars in their driveway and the lights in their windows and once even caught a glimpse of him in an upstairs room.

It had to happen. I knew it had to happen.

The days you were most likely to see his car, I'd worked out, were Tuesdays and Wednesdays, and one Wednesday, as I kept Tanya hanging about at the end of her road, Mr Knox's Alfa Romeo finally pulled up at the lights.

He was right beside us. Metres away. It was real. It was happening. For a moment, I couldn't breathe. 'There he is,' I said, and Tanya followed my gaze and said, 'No, wise up, what are you doing?'

'Mr Knox!' I yelled, and I waved at the car. 'Mr Knox!'

His windows were wound halfway down – he was smoking – and he ducked to look out, then pressed a button to wind them down fully. 'Hello?' he said. 'What is it, is everything okay?'

'Mr Knox,' I said, 'we need a lift, will you give us a lift?'

'Stop it!' Tanya hissed at me.

'Please, Mr Knox!' I said. 'We're really late and it's important.'

The lights were still red, but any moment they'd go amber, and green.

'Please, Mr Knox,' I said. 'You have to, please, you have to.' I had taken to wearing a dab of Poison every day I had a French or Spanish lesson – even though Lisa told me I was a weirdo – and I could still smell the perfume, Davina's perfume, on me, and I wondered if he could too, creeping from me in a slow green spiral.

He took a drag of his cigarette and dropped it out of the window. 'Where are you going?'

Tanya hissed again and grabbed my arm, but I wrenched it free. The lights were amber, and, as they turned green, I was opening the passenger seat and getting in. There I was, in Mr Knox's Alfa Romeo. It was happening.

'Where do you need to go?' he said again, and I said, 'Anywhere.' He looked at me and raised an eyebrow and snorted with laughter, and I thought he might tell me to get out, but he didn't, he just revved the engine and then accelerated away, and in the wing mirror I caught a glimpse of Tanya's stricken face, open-mouthed, and I looked at Mr Knox beside me – Mr Knox, I was there, now, finally, in Mr Knox's car, me and Mr Knox – and I started laughing too.

Afterwards, I couldn't resist telling Tanya. I told her how he kissed me, gently at first, and his lips were soft. Then harder, with his tongue. I told her how he undid my tie and unbuttoned my shirt, and how his fingers were cool on my skin. I told her how he slipped his hand underneath my skirt and traced his fingertips up, then hooked his fingers under my panties and tugged them down.

'He didn't,' she said, big-eyed and scared, and I promised her, 'Yes, he did.' And her shock spurred me on, and I said how it hurt at the start. I said there was blood. I said it was in the back seat of his Alfa Romeo, in a cul-de-sac near the golf club, and he'd spread his jacket out first and afterwards he'd smoked a cigarette.

Once I'd told Tanya, I had to tell Donna, and Lisa, and when Lisa looked at me with slitted eyes and said I was lying, I got out the condom and showed them: as proof, I said, he'd given it me for next time.

I hadn't counted on Tanya blubbering it all to her mother – all of it, including the time we went to his house. We got in such trouble for that, but the trouble he was in was worse.

Even though I cracked as soon as my mum asked me, told her that I'd made it all up, she didn't believe me, couldn't understand why I'd make it up or how I'd even know what to make up in the first place. In a series of anguished phone calls, she and Tanya's mother decided Mr Knox had an unhealthy hold over me, over all of us.

There's no smoke, they agreed, without fire.

They contacted the headmistress, and that was that: Mr Knox was called before the governors and forced to resign, and I was sent to a counsellor who tried to make me talk about my parents' divorce. And then, in the autumn, we heard that Davina had left Mr Knox, had taken her babies and gone back to her mother's. It must have been her worst

nightmare come true, the merest suggestion that her husband, the father of her two children, would do it again. She,
more than anyone else, would have known there was no
such thing as innocence.

I think she was right.

I don't believe it was a one-off.

What happened that day is that he drove me five minutes up the road, then pulled a U-turn at the garage and
drove back down the other side and made me get out not
far from where he'd picked me up and said, 'Now this was
a one-off, you know,' and laughed. But I can still see his
expression as he dropped me off: the half-smile, the eyebrow raised even as he said it wasn't to happen again.

It had happened before. And there's a certain intensity
that only a fourteen- or fifteen-year-old girl can possess: I
would have redoubled my efforts at snaring him. If only I
hadn't told Tanya.

★

I lifted my glass of wine and took a sip, and then another.
Mr Knox and Melissa were still giggling over the cocktail
menu, flicking back and forth through the pages. 'Excuse
me,' I said, turning to the bar and addressing the nearest barman. He didn't hear me, carried on carving twists of orange
peel. 'Excuse me,' I said again, louder. He raised his finger:
one moment. But I carried on. 'You see the couple over
there? By the window? The man with the black hair and the
blonde girl?' He frowned and put the orange down, looked

at them, then back at me. 'Can I pay for their drinks?' I blurted.

'You'd like to buy them a drink?'

'Yes, whatever they're having. All of it. I want to pay for all of it.'

'I'll just get the bar manager for you. One moment, please.'

My heart was pounding. It was impulsive, and utterly stupid. My friends hadn't even arrived yet, we'd still be sitting here when Mr Knox asked for his bill in a drink or so's time, and how would I explain it to them, or to him, because the barman would point me out as the one who'd paid for it. Even if I asked them not to let on, not to give me away, my name would be on the credit-card slip, so he'd know. Or would he? Would my name mean anything to him, all these years later? Surely it would. Surely it must.

I swivelled on my stool to look at them again. Melissa, with her blonde hair and pouting glossy lips and blue eyes, didn't look very much like him. She didn't look much like Davina either, come to that. They were mock-arguing about something now. She flicked her hair and cocked her head and put her hands on her waist, a pantomime of indignation, and he took her bare upper arms and squeezed them, shaking her lightly, and she squealed, then threw her head back in laughter as he leant in to murmur something in her ear.

She had to be his daughter. She had to be.

'Ma'am, excuse me?' The bar manager was leaning across the bar, attempting to get my attention. 'Excuse me?'

'Sorry,' I said. 'I was miles away.'

She had to be his daughter.

'I understand you'd like to buy a drink for the cou͟ by the window?'

'No,' I said. 'I'm sorry, I was mistaken. I mean, I thought they were someone else.'

'No problem,' he said, smooth, professional. 'Is there anything else I can do for you?'

I looked at him. He waited, head politely inclined. I almost asked, 'Can you find out their names?' Then I realised that, either way, I didn't want to know.

Escape Routes

FOR MOST OF THAT YEAR, you are obsessed with slipways and secret ways through Zork. Not cheats, which suddenly give you the treasures without your having to earn them – they're something else entirely. What you mean – what Christopher calls them – is wormholes. Places where it looks like you're stuck and then squirm through to safety, whisked through space and time. The first, and best, is in the Altar Room:

```
In one corner
```

it says,

```
is a small black hole which leads to darkness.
```

You haven't a prayer of getting the coffin down there.

For weeks, you've tried to find another way back, discarding all of your hard-won items as you go: the nasty knife, the garlic, the bottle of water, even the jewelled egg, because the voice keeps on saying that you're carrying too much. You've run through all the verbs you know, and have looked up others. Push coffin! Squeeze coffin! Shrink! Dismantle! Coerce! But none of them works. Then one night Christopher tells you the wormhole is 'Pray'. You blink at him.

Type it, he says, stringing his hair behind his ears. Go on. Type 'pray'.

You type it, and then next thing you're back in the forest, coffin and all.

You see? he says, and when you say, How did you know? he just shrugs and smiles.

Christopher's not like the other babysitters. They like to get you and your brother off to bed as soon as possible so they can eat their pizza and watch TV and phone their friends. You listen in, sometimes, on the extension in your parents' room, the handset tilted away from your face, the mouthpiece muffled. Their conversations follow the same, set patterns, over and over and on and on, and mostly you get bored before they finish. But it's never boring with Christopher. He brings over floppy disks of games, Kix and Deathstar, Repton, Bonecruncher, Labyrinth and Snapper, a different selection each time, and he sits on the floor with you beside the BBC computer and tells you when to duck and where to turn and what to avoid, and when the Deathstar's coming, he takes over while you hide your eyes. Zork, which is your best game, he gave to you for your tenth birthday, for you to play whenever you want. He tells your parents it's a series of verbal reasoning and logistical puzzles and because of this they let you play it almost as much as you want, instead of limiting it to twenty minutes after your homework and piano practice is done.

By the entrance to Hades and the Desolation, where the voices lament and the evil spirits jeer – the next place you get stuck – you try Christopher's wormhole again.

```
>Pray
```

you command.

```
If you pray hard enough, your prayers might be
answered.
```

Your heart leaps.

```
>Pray hard
```

you try.

```
I don't know the word 'hard'.
```

So again you try 'pray', and 'pray', and 'pray pray pray', and 'pray the Lord's Prayer' and 'pray with all my heart'. But it doesn't work this time. Then you try typing 'pray' repeatedly, over forty-one times, you count, until your fingers are in spasms and the screen no longer seems to be moving. But the wormhole is closed, and even the thesaurus – Adjure! Beseech! Implore! Solicit! – is no good. The next time you see him, you tell Christopher about this, and he says suddenly, Do you believe in prayer?

You don't know what he means, and he says, In life?

We pray in school, you say. At the end of Assembly, the Lord's Prayer, every morning.

Do you believe in it? he says. In God?

No, you say. I don't know. Maybe. Your mum and dad are atheists, which is unusual, and he knows this, and this is why he asked. You've been to church four times that you remember: for Brown Owl's wedding and for carols at Christmas. Christopher is intrigued by this. He's writing an essay, he tells you, on faith and whether it's acquired or innate. He tells you of children raised by wolves, then found by humans; he talks about men making paintings with red clay and sticks on the walls of hidden caves. You don't understand what he's saying, but you listen, or pretend to, because you like Christopher, and he doesn't normally talk so much.

Christopher is studying Philosophy at Queen's, plays guitar and likes Japanese girls, or so he says, though his on-off girlfriend Kathryn has a round reddish face and limp blonde hair and isn't even remotely Japanese. You don't like Kathryn. Sometimes when Christopher is babysitting she comes too, and she sits on the sofa with her magazine and expects him to sit beside her and huffs loud sighs if you ask him to help with a tricky level. She's always asking him to cut his hair, too, and he never does, and she gets cross about it. He's got long hair, longer than yours, which he wears centre-parted and tucked behind his ears, tied into a ponytail at the neck, and she says it's disgusting on a man. She says to him, Even your own mother says the same, for goodness' sake. But your mum says, Good on him, he's unafraid to be an individual instead of following the herd.

As Christopher talks, blinking and waggling his hands, you wonder what it would be like to kiss him, like Kathryn does, mouths and lips. The thought of it used to gross you out. But recently it's been making you jittery, a hollow feeling in your stomach that you don't quite understand.

The summer Christopher goes missing, you only see him twice.

While things are uncertain, during the summer months, your parents rarely go out. The second-last time, his mother and yours get stuck across town – a funeral, and then some kind of scare, the bridges closed – and he takes you and your brother back to his. He's looking after a puppy for a friend, and his mum is worried it'll have the utility room destroyed if it's left alone too long – your mothers were only supposed to be gone for a couple of hours.

The puppy is mostly miniature Schnauzer with maybe a dash of something else: it has whiskers and a fringe and a face like a little old man. At six months old, it's still too small for its paws. When you get there, it's whimpering and crying, pressing into the gap between the tumble-drier and the wall. It takes ten minutes and a trail of doggy chocolate buttons to entice it out, while Christopher mixes bleach in a pail and mops up its puddles. Once it's out, you pet and cuddle it like a baby, and eventually it starts to get bolder, yipping and nipping at your fingers, and then the three of you take it out into the garden for a game of chase.

After a while, you need the toilet and go inside. The house is a bungalow, with the bedrooms and guest bathroom off one long corridor. On your way back, you pause at the door of Christopher's room. It's slightly ajar, and you tell yourself that you're not spying because the door was open anyway, and before you know it you've slipped inside and you're standing in his bedroom.

Although you've been to the house many times, you've never been inside this room. It smells musty and herbal, forbidden. The curtains are closed, even though it's daytime, but there's enough light leaking through for you to see: the rumpled unmade bed, the guitars propped up against the far wall, the balled-up socks and the shed skins of T-shirts.

You take a tiny step inside, and another. Glued to the walls, and the wardrobe doors, and even covering most of the inside wardrobe mirror, are pictures of bands, and one band in particular, a band you know Christopher loves: the Manic Street Preachers. The biggest picture is ripped from a newspaper, and it shows a man with letters carved into his arm: actually carved, with angry rough slashes of a knife. You trace them out: 4 REAL they say. There's a fluttery feeling in your stomach, a giddy, hot-sick feeling, and you are slightly breathless as you squint at the newsprint reporting that Richey Edwards went missing on the day—

A noise outside makes you jump, and you realise it's the back door slamming: the others coming in. You slip from the room, taking care to leave the door exactly as it was, and go back to meet them in the kitchen, your heart opening and closing in your chest like a fist.

Two weeks later, the last time you see him, Christopher promises not to tell when he finds you and Alison McKeag from down the road smoking ripped-up sachets of bouquet garni wrapped in loo roll out of the bathroom window. He just laughs and says so long as you stick to smoking herbs you're fine, it's tobacco that's evil, and tobacco companies. Then he says, God it really stinks in here you know, but before you panic about your parents, he helps to push the window open past its paint-stiff hinge and wash the flakes down the sink, and he gets a can of Lynx from his bag to spray to hide the smell. You just say it was me, he says, if they say anything. Say I was meeting Kathryn afterwards and wanted to freshen up.

Are you? you ask, a bit cheekily, emboldened by the presence of Alison McKeag. He looks at you. No, he says. We broke up last week.

Sorry, you say, not knowing what to say, and Alison titters. Was it you dumped her? she says, flicking a glance at you sideways, Or did she dump you?

Christopher unhooks his wire-rimmed glasses and rubs them on the corner of his tartan shirt. Then he puts them back on and looks at you, steadily, as he answers. Dump is an ugly word, he says, because it presumes that people are garbage, worthless. I don't think it's right to ever talk about dumping people.

Beside you, Alison is pretending to be struggling not to giggle. You can already hear her, down the bus-stop by the shops, tomorrow or the following afternoon, the way she'll make his voice high-pitched and pompous and imitate the ponytail and the glasses. Already you know too that you'll go along with it, because you'll have to.

I'm going to put the pizza on, Christopher says, after a pause that stretches too long. Do you two want any?

No, says Alison, and then she links your arm and says, Us two are away to talk about girly things, aren't we?

Yeah, you say, and you try to make your eyes say sorry, but Christopher just smiles and says, Fair play.

Later, when Alison's gone, you find him sitting on the sofa, just sitting, the TV not even on. Your brother's oblivious, playing Deathstar next door, squealing and yelping along with the beeps.

Do you want to play Zork? you say. I've got to a new bit I'm stuck on.

Once you've booted your brother off the two of you play for more than an hour. Christopher tells you the trick is not just to take the sceptre but to wave it: 'wave sceptre'. Not a wormhole, exactly, but something you'd never have thought of – and suddenly the rainbow is solid. Not now, but later, he says, you'll need to walk over it. For the moment, he says, look around, and you 'look around', and there, where there wasn't before, is a pot of gold.

Hey!, you say, but he just says, South-west now, and all the way back to Canyon View. Then north-west to the Clearing and west back to the Window and into the

Kitchen and west again back to the Living Room to put your treasures into the case.

Why are you telling me this? you ask, because normally – unless you're about to be killed – he lets you work it out for yourself. There's three more parts, he says, and this is only Part I, although it's taken you months to work out how to make it this far.

How do you know all this anyway? you say then, annoyed. He just shrugs, and plucks at the rubber band keeping back his hair. Are you sad about Kathryn? you suddenly say, looking away from him back at the screen and feeling your face rush hot.

Am I sad about Kathryn? he says in a way that sounds like a no but could be a yes, and you don't know how to ask again. Maybe you'll meet someone Japanese next time, you think of saying, but there are no Japanese people in Belfast. So you say nothing and just make your way through the forest again as he watches.

You finish Part I and diligently play a week's worth of Part II, wanting to surprise him with how far you've got, drowning again and again in the maintenance room of the dam until you work out not to push the blue button, just the yellow. In the end, though, you never get further than this, because that's when he goes missing.

Your parents tell you, calmly. He'll turn up, they say. He's probably with friends in Glasgow, that's what Kathryn's suggested, and he's got a schoolfriend in Manchester too, so they're checking that out next. It's only been a week.

He's old enough to look after himself. He'll surely turn up soon.

They don't know that you've listened to his mother on the other end of the phone, picking up the extension more carefully than you've ever done before and hardly daring to breathe, your palm damp over the mouthpiece. You've heard her gulps and sobs as your mother tries to comfort her. You know he didn't leave a note, but you know he didn't take anything either: not the jar of fifty-pence pieces on his shelf, not his beloved guitar, not his Discman, not even — so far as they can tell — a change of clothes or underwear. You want to speak up and ask her if maybe he's in Tokyo, but of course you can't do that, and, anyway, you don't really believe it yourself.

One night you have a nightmare that he's trapped in Zork and after that you find you can no longer play it because the voice that instructs and responds, making wise-cracks and not understanding, suddenly sounds too much like his. The thought that he's in there, trying to talk to you, makes your skin tighten and crawl, and you take out the disk and shove it back in its sleeve and bury it right at the back of the box. You think of the pictures on his wardrobe, and you think that the whole year of Zork was a training in the secret messages that people are trying to tell you, that are there to be read, if only you know how. And you know then, you just know, that he's never coming back.

Killing Time

I TRY TO KILL MYSELF ON THE FIRST OF MARCH, a Sunday. I haven't planned it. I somehow just find myself standing in the bathroom, my heart beating fast, watching the watery light through the rippled windowpanes, knowing I'm going to, and suddenly it all makes sense. I kneel to reach right to the back of the cabinet under the sink where the medicines are kept, rooting through plasters and sanitary towels and sticky bottles of herbal cough syrup, and next thing I'm sitting cross-legged on my bed pushing the paracetamol tablets from the blister pack, shaking out what there is of baby aspirin, until there is a little heap that I line up on the duvet.

I have no idea about the dosage. My mum, a keep-fit addict and health freak, doesn't believe in painkillers except in the direst of emergencies. My brother and I have grown up on clove oil for toothaches, arnica for bruises and camomile tea for upset stomachs. She buys the camomile flowers in dusty bags from Nature's Way on the Upper Newtownards Road, along with dried feverfew leaves for her headaches and Chinese tea that is meant to be an appetite suppressant. I tried it once: it is thin and bitter and brown-tasting and makes your tongue feel dry in your mouth.

My mouth is dry now. Time is catching and skipping, and yet I've been methodical enough to fill the toothbrush mug with water and bring it back into my bedroom with me. I lift it and take a sip. The lip is thick, and the water inside is slimy and mint-edged. But I don't trust myself to go downstairs and get a proper glass or even to go to the bathroom to rinse out the tooth mug and refill it. I swallow and try to read the instructions on the paracetamol packet. Children below the age of twelve, it says, should have no more than four tablets in twenty-four hours. Adults can have up to eight. There are eight tablets left, and I have only just turned thirteen. Taking them all at once must surely make a difference too. I study the baby aspirin packaging. It is cherry-flavoured, chewable and years out of date. The most it can do, I decide, is nothing. I straighten one of the tablets on the duvet, aligning it with its partner. There is a sort of ringing in my ears. I take another sip of the swampy water. Then I begin to swallow down the paracetamol, a pair at a time. A song starts playing in my head: part of a song, a silly nursery rhyme from years ago. The animals went in two by two, hurrah, hurrah. I swallow the final pair of paracetamol. The elephant and the kangaroo. The baby aspirin are sharp and taste nothing like cherries. I have to stop myself spitting them back out. I sit for a moment. The song and its animals are parading around my head, over and over, their thumping insistent feet. The unicorn got there just too late for to get out of the rain. I brush the trail of white dust from the duvet and get up. I look at my face in the mirror. My fringe needs cutting. I take the tooth mug back to the bathroom and carefully replace the toothbrushes in it, bright and stiff on their plastic stalks. Then I brush my teeth to get rid of the synthetic taste and return to my bedroom and lie down on the bed.

This autumn, we studied *The Crucible* in English. For months I haven't been able to stop thinking about the scene where Giles Corey refuses to answer ay or nay and so is pressed to death. *Peine forte et dure*, it was called, where they laid you down and stone after stone was put on your chest until under the weight of it you could no longer breathe. Sometimes it took minutes, but sometimes it took days. Giles Corey, the real Giles Corey, was an actual person. He was the only person in the whole of the United States to die by pressing, but they used to do it in the UK and France all the time. I looked it up in an encyclopedia in the library after school. The first day you were allowed bread; the second and subsequent days, foul water.

There was a difference, Miss Gibson said, between saying that someone died and someone was killed. Saying that someone died was a way of reneging on your responsibility if in fact they had been killed, or murdered. She wrote it on the blackboard, 'to renege on', and underlined it. Then she wrote beside it a ladder of words, from 'murdered' at the top to 'passed away' at the bottom. We were to be alert to the strengths words had and, most of all, to their shadows – the ways you could use them to mean or to not mean something, or to wriggle out of having to say something directly. We should listen to the news with our eyes closed, she said, so that we could hear more clearly. A few girls giggled when she said that. She pretended she didn't notice, but a web of colour inched across her face. Ashleigh McAuley said that when she turned away to put the books back in the store cupboard she was crying. *Peine forte et dure.* You could feel the weight of the stones as you said it, each of them.

An hour or so later, my father calls me down for dinner, and I sit up, straighten my fringe with my fingers, tighten my ponytail and go downstairs. We sit there, the four of us, forking potatoes and nut roast, the scrape of knives on china, asking and answering questions about school, friends, neighbours. Afterwards, I go back up to my room and get into bed again, still fully clothed. I close my eyes and try to breathe. I can't tell if my liver hurts or even, when I think about it, where it is supposed to be hurting. I read the back of the packaging again, and all of the small print in the leaflet inside. I assumed an overdose would make you drift off into a marshmallowy sleep, but paracetamol isn't designed to send you to sleep so it must be your liver. Or maybe your kidneys. I'm not sure of the difference: all we've done in Science so far this year is food chains and plant reproduction. Carpels and anthers and stamens. I got good marks because my drawings were so neat, and I'd colour-coordinated them.

I lie there. I listen to the sounds of the TV, shrunken and muffled through the ceiling and carpet. I listen to my dad taking Sheba out to the back garden. My bedroom is right above them so I hear him talking to her, calling her Sheebs and Shub-Shub and Old Girl, teasing her about next-door's cat, who Sheba's terrified of. I hear her bark, as if they're having a conversation, and the sound of the door slamming as they go back inside.

I know that two hours have passed when 'Boogie Nights' starts playing: my mum does her Rosemary Conley video every morning and evening but you have to wait at least two hours after meals. Sometimes I do it with her. *One two three four five six seven eight.* And out. The video finishes, and then it's Sheba to the garden one last time and doors being locked and footsteps on stairs and calls of 'Goodnight!' The taps running, the toilet flushing. 'Goodnight!' my little brother's piping voice. 'Goodnight!'

I lie awake for a long, long while. Eventually, I somehow sleep.

And, to my surprise, I wake up, and things go on as usual: school, viola practice, homework. I tidy my room and learn my French vocab. The weird thing is I feel better than I have done in ages. It's like a safety valve has been released, and for the first time I can breathe again. Monday, Tuesday, Wednesday, Thursday, Friday. The week passes. It's sort of as if things matter less now, and, because they matter less, they are more bearable.

On Saturday, my parents have a wedding reception to go to, a late lunch at the Park Avenue – a friend of theirs who got divorced and is now remarrying. They've decided we're old enough, for the first time ever, to be left home alone: it's during the daytime, after all, and only down the road. They leave just after two. I watch the taxi pull away from the kerb and turn onto the main road and give them five minutes in case they've forgotten something. Then I yell out to Niall to stay in his room and not to move until I get back.

It's a wet, blustery day, not a day to be outside. But it's been burning my mind all week, and I might not get another chance.

I walk fast, through the residential streets, my collar pulled up for warmth – and to hide my face. It is only a ten-minute walk to the main road and the shops, but I've never felt so visible, so naked. Cars whoosh past, some with their headlights on already, spraying dirty puddled water up onto the pavement. Every time a car sounds its horn or backfires in the distance I nearly jump out of my skin. Our parents laid down the law before they left: no fighting, no answering the door and absolutely no going out, under any circumstances. My mum panics about us when she doesn't know where we are.

It's a relief to reach the newsagent's, push open the door to the sound of the bell and the babble of voices and the steamy warm fug. 'What can I do you for?' the newsagent says when my turn comes. He is a nice man: Mick, and his wife is Alanna. I suddenly think that despite everything I should have gone elsewhere, somewhere up in Ballyhackamore, further afield.

I take a breath. I hope he can't see the weird guilt I feel written on my face. As soon as the painkillers are back in the cupboard, I tell myself, it will be like nothing ever happened. 'I need a packet of paracetamol,' I say.

'Well, you're out of luck,' he says, winking over my head at the old man shuffling up behind me. 'And do you know why that is?' I blink at him. 'Because the parrots in the jungle have them all eaten. Parrots-eat-'em-all: d'you get me?' The old man behind me hacks out a phlegmy laugh. Mick looks disappointed that I haven't laughed. I force a smile. He reaches behind him and takes a box from the shelf. They're a different kind than the ones we had, but I hope that by the time they come to need it my parents won't notice.

'Anything else?' Mick says.

'A bottle of baby aspirin?'

'No can do. Don't stock it, only the normal stuff.'

I'll have to do without the baby aspirin. But that's okay: they can't have used it since Niall was wee; they've probably forgotten it was even there. The paracetamol's the main thing. I hand over fifty pence, and he rings up my change.

'How many,' I hear myself saying, and the words come out of nowhere, 'how many can you take at once?'

Mick frowns, and picks up the packet. 'Says here no more than four doses in twenty-four hours.'

'And four doses is eight tablets?'

'That's what it says. These for yourself, love?'

'They're . . . for my mum. Her headache. She gets these headaches.'

The old man leans forward and taps my shoulder. 'You'd want to be careful, but,' he says.

'I'm sorry?' I say.

'I said, you'd want to be careful, but.'

I turn to look at him. His face is thin and lined, and his eyes are milky, and there are plugs of yellowish-white hair in his ears. He puts his face right up to me, and I can feel his warm, wet breath.

'Woman the wife knew,' he says, leaning in even closer, 'got this terrible headache. Kept popping the pills, every couple of hours. Headache passes, she thinks no more of it, goes about her business. Few days later, the vomiting starts, and her skin turns yellow. Then she swells up like your Michelin Man. By the time they got her to hospital, it was too late.'

'What do you mean?' I say. I try to take a step back, only my back's right against the counter, and there's nowhere to go. 'What do you mean?'

'She'd OD'd, you see,' he says, flecking me with spittle. 'She'd overdosed. It had her liver and whatnot destroyed, and her organs were packing it in one after the other. Oh, you wouldn't wish it on your worst enemy, what that poor woman went through. It's the most painful way to go, they say, for they can't give you anything to help with the pain once your liver's packed in. And the tragedy is she done it without realising. Her family was in pieces. In pieces. A *Telegraph*, Mick, and a packet of B&H, if you please.'

I stare at the old man. He looks like . . . what's the word? A harbinger.

'Is that true?' I say.

'Sorry, dear?'

'Is it true – what you said? About the woman.'

'God rest her soul. It was a terrible tragedy. Terrible.'

'And it was definitely the painkillers, it wasn't anything else?'

'Oh aye, it was the headache pills for sure. They should come with more warnings, if you ask me. The cruellest part is she thought she was fine. The headache lifted, and she was right as rain for days. Or so she thought. When all the while the damage was being done. God rest her soul.'

His milky eyes glide over my face again, searching to meet mine. A great rush of heat and then cold goes through my body.

'Don't be scaremongering there, Eddie,' says Mick. 'You've put the heart crossways in the wee girl, look at her face.'

'I wish it was only scaremongering,' the old man says. 'They say it happens oftener than you'd think. They should put warnings on the packets. You wouldn't wish it on your worst enemy.'

'Come on, Eddie. I'm sure her mum knows what she's doing. Don't mind him, love. Now then.' Mick rings up the till. The old man is still peering at me. He knows, I think. I don't know how, but he knows. I squeeze past him and manage to get out of the shop and into the dank fag-end of an alleyway around the corner.

I try to tell myself the old man was mad, or lying. I scrabble to recall what we did in Home Economics, when we studied first aid. Don't touch someone you suspect has been electrocuted. Never use butter to treat a burn. ABC stands for Airways Breathing Circulation. The rules ping, neat and useless, around my head. We didn't mention painkiller overdose. The closest we came was when Mrs McAneary was talking about tying a tourniquet, and Kelly Clark put up her hand and asked was it true that cutting your wrists across didn't work, you had to cut them down? Mrs McAneary told her not to be so morbid and if there was any more of that sort of talk she'd be in detention.

I feel a kind of numbness come over my body. I put a hand on one of the dustbin lids to steady myself. I try to think logically. I try to think Miss Gibson-style. A few days later, the old man said. How many is a few? Three, four? Surely no more than five? A couple is two or three, and several might be longer, but a few days, surely, has to be less than a week, has to be fewer than – what has it been? – six days.

Slowly, I calm myself down. It is raining more heavily now, and I'm getting soaked, but I stay there in the vomit-spattered alleyway until my legs feel strong enough to take me back home.

I go up the Holywood Road this time. As I pass the Park Avenue, I suddenly think about going inside, up the driveway and into the lobby and through to the restaurant, finding my parents. But what would I say? There's nothing, whatever I say, that my parents can do. I stand across the road looking at the gates of the hotel, my hands clenched into fists so tight that blood wells up in half-moons under the skin where my nails dig in. When I wrench myself away it feels as if years might have passed.

When I make it home, Niall is in his room, the door shut, a skull-and-crossboned NO GIRLS ALLOWED sign Blu-tacked up. In smaller letters he's written, 'and that means you!!!'

I tap on the door.

'Go away,' he says. 'I'm busy.'

'Niall,' I say, nudging the door open a crack. He's hunched over, gluing something.

'I thought you were meant to be good at English,' he says. 'Can you not read?'

'Niall,' I say, but the words won't come out.

'What?' he says.

'Niall,' I try again.

'*What?*' he says, and when I don't reply, he rolls his eyes and goes back to his gluing. 'Give my head peace.'

'Do you want to play Lego?' I blurt out.

He stares at me. 'Do I what?'

'Do you want to play Lego? We could build the Pirate Ship and the Space Rocket, have a battle.'

Niall shifts in his chair and looks at me.

'It'll be epic,' I say. 'It'll be huge. It'll be like . . . carnage.'

'I don't know,' he says. 'I don't really play with Lego these days.'

'Since when?' I say. 'Not even the Pirate Ship?' It was his Christmas present the year before last, and even I was jealous of it.

'I don't know,' he says. 'I just don't. Sheba ate some of the pieces anyway, I think.'

'Oh,' I say.

'Not that I care anyway,' he says, turning back to his gluing, 'but if I tell Mum and Dad you went out, you're in such big trouble.'

'Niall?' I say, and I hear my voice crack a little. 'I don't know what to do.'

He frowns at me. 'Do you mean, like, now?'

'Now – for the rest of the day – please Niall – can I sit in here with you?' I say, and my voice is barely a whisper now. 'I won't get in your way, I promise.'

'Wise up,' he says. Then he sighs. 'Look,' he says, pushing his cardboard to one side. 'You can watch me play Paperboy if you want. I almost got a Perfect Delivery the other day on Middle Road.'

When I try to thank him, he looks at me like I've gone mad, so I shut up and just follow him downstairs.

We boot up the Amstrad and sit side by side while he fires the newspapers at the doors and crashes into flowerpots and dodges the stray rolling tyres and remote-controlled cars and tornadoes. It's banal and repetitive and weirdly hypnotic. Gradually, I feel my breathing lengthen and my heartbeat slow. I stop watching the computer screen after a while and watch Niall instead, his pale, creased forehead, his flicking thumbs. We sit there for hours. By the time he gives up on the elusive Perfect Delivery it's almost teatime, so I micro-wave the jacket potatoes Mum has left cling-filmed in the fridge, three minutes each plate, and grate cheese carefully over. Niall eats his and most of mine. After we've finished, I do the washing-up, drying each knife and fork individually, eking them out. *So long as you keep moving*, I say to myself. It's like in the game: you can speed up or slow down but you have to keep moving, because as soon as you stop, it's over. I line up the last knife in its compartment and close the cutlery drawer. Niall is back up in his room by now, at work on whatever he's cutting and gluing. I wet the dishcloth and wipe the table, then wring it out and drape it over the tap. I am more tired than I can ever remember being, more tired than I even knew was possible. I want to go to bed, but I don't dare – in case I don't wake up this time.

As I wonder what to do next, I hear Sheba whine by the back door and I realise we haven't let her out all afternoon. 'Come on then,' I say, and she gives a little thump of her tail, or tries to. I unlock the door, and she hauls herself up and pads outside. The rain still hasn't let up. She makes it across the yard and to the edge of the garden and squats: to make her puddle, I suddenly think, that's what we always used to call it when we were little. I don't remember a time without Sheba. I don't remember when she was a puppy, except in photographs. She's always just been there.

She shambles back to the house, and I let her in and kneel down on the floor beside her. She was really blonde once, platinum-bright, but now she's kind of an ashy colour, and her muzzle is grey. She's getting on: that's what my parents say. Poor old Sheba's getting on. I stroke her and see how knotted her undercoat is. So I tease her soft drifts of tummy fur until they untangle and brush through her damp topcoat with my fingers. It isn't dirty, exactly, because she doesn't go outside much any more, but it doesn't feel clean. She's too stiff and cumbersome to climb into the bath, and it seems cruel to blast her with a cold hose in the middle of winter, so she hasn't been properly bathed for weeks. My dad wipes her down with a facecloth and soapy water from time to time, but she needs a proper shampoo. Maybe we could all make a sort of hammock, I suddenly think, out of a sheet, and all four of us could lift her into the bath and out. I could blow dry her coat afterwards, on the lowest gentle setting, so she doesn't get a chill.

Maybe we could do it tomorrow afternoon: maybe that's what we could do. And by then a whole week would have passed, seven whole days, and that was surely more than a few, and then I'd know I'd made it safely through. Surely a week was enough surely? I curl up with Sheba, there on the linoleum tiles of the utility-room floor, and close my eyes and breathe in her warm, sour, biscuity smell, exhausted suddenly with something almost like relief.

The rest of March passes. March turns into April, and in the middle of April Easter comes, and on Easter Monday Sheba dies. Mum bought her doggy chocolates from Supermac, but she didn't eat them, only licked at them and wagged the tip of her tail, and the next morning she's stiff and cold against the utility-room door. We all cry, even Dad.

Later that night, I hear my parents talking on the landing. Niall has been inconsolable all day, and Mum's had to sit with him until he's sobbed himself to sleep. 'It's good for them,' she says. 'That's what they say. It teaches them about mortality.' But she's crying as she says it — I can hear. Then she says, 'That's a joke. Isn't that a fucking joke?' Mum never swears. I have never in my life, ever, heard Mum say anything stronger than 'sugar' or 'flipping' or 'fudge'. I hear Dad shush and soothe her, as if he's the only parent and she is a child.

I think of the things they said to each other and to us when we found Sheba this morning. 'She's gone to sleep'; 'She's passed away'; 'She's gone to a better place'. They are all gentle, cloudy phrases. Right at the other end of the scale from 'murdered', 'killed' or even 'died'. And somewhere off the scale entirely is the poisonous word for what I tried to do. I try to make myself whisper it aloud, but I can't: the word just sits on my tongue, too terrible to say. Miss Gibson didn't so much as mention it when she wrote out her ladder of death words.

As I lie in bed, I listen to them on the landing and wonder. I try not to, but I still can't stop wondering, how many more tablets it would have taken: another whole strip of eight, or maybe four, or maybe only two or even one. For a sudden long moment I can't seem to breathe. And then I breathe; and then I concentrate only on breathing.

Through the Wardrobe

It starts with the Belle dress.

Your mum takes you all to the store in Donegall Place the week it opens, braving the lashing rain in the queue outside, all of you jumping and shivering with cold and excitement. Inside is the most magical place you've ever seen. Your sisters go hopping and squealing to the cuddly toys at the back, heaped right to the ceiling, but you just stand, clutching your mum's hand, unable to move or even to breathe. It is like being in Heaven, or outer space – somewhere far away from the grey November street and dirty puddles outside.

The shop is dim, lit by hundreds of pinpricks of light, like stars. Music is playing: 'Part of Your World', from *The Little Mermaid*. This is the part where Ariel and Flounder twirl and somersault and swim to the very top of the cavern, while Sebastian freaks out at his own reflection and gets trapped in a tankard.

You've seen that film so many times you know each word of it by heart, and this is your best scene, better even than when Ariel rescues the Prince. Your oldest sister likes to tell you it's not what happens in reality, but your mum says not to listen to her.

You grip your mum's hand even tighter. Go on, your mum says. Go on, and she prises your fingers from hers. It is only a few weeks till Christmas, Santa's elves will be watching. You take a step in, and then another. There are tables and tables of toys, plush and soft and shiny and gleaming, but it's the costumes you're staring at: the princess dresses. They hang, shimmering, from racks just above your head. There is Tinkerbell, with gauzy wings, and there's Snow White, and there is Aurora, from *Sleeping Beauty*. There is Belle, from *Beauty and the Beast*. You've never played at being Belle before. But the Belle dress is the most beautiful thing you've seen. It has frothy pink straps and a velvet rose in the centre of the chest; its tight bodice billows into a full skirt, gathered at the front with six pink bows. The Belle dress is a bright shimmery yellow and in the soft light it looks like gold. You know how it would feel to dance in that dress: it would feel like being wrapped in a sunbeam. It would be impossible to be sad in that dress.

You are sad. You're only six years old, but you feel sad a lot of the time, a tightness in your chest that you don't have words for. Your mum says you're a sensitive child. Your dad says you've too many older sisters. Your dad says your mum babies you. Your mum says shh, she'll stay there till you fall asleep, you're safe and nothing can hurt you. But it's not outside you're scared of. It's something inside, and you can't explain it, but you know, just know, that in the dress you'd be safe from it.

All of a sudden, your sisters are clustering round, a hundred arms plucking and tugging, yanking the dresses off hangers to hold them up and laugh and strike poses, squabbling over who saw what first, who bagsies which. Look at this, your mum says, crouching beside you, and she shows you an Aladdin costume, complete with a plastic scimitar; then Peter Pan's green tunic and cap with a feather. Your eldest sister seizes the cap and squashes it onto your head – Look at the wee dote! – and everyone looks at you, even the shop assistants, with their lilac and mint-green polo-shirts and jaunty visors and wide matching grins, and you feel your cheeks surge red.

Your earliest memory: wanting to push your willy between your legs as you sat on the toilet, and your father getting frustrated and setting you on your feet, showing you how to aim at the back of the bowl, and your mum saying, Don't be cross with him, Alan.

You long for the Belle dress so much it makes you feel sick. You tidy your toys and make your bed and eat every last scrap on your plate, even when it is broccoli. What's the difference between broccoli and bogeys? your dad says. Kids don't eat broccoli. Your sisters say, That's gross, and, Eeew. Your dad elbows you in the ribs, pretends to punch your shoulder. You wriggle away. Your mum says, Alan.

You make desperate deals with Santa in your head: you'll never ask for anything again, ever, if you can have that dress. It can count for next Christmas too, and the one after that.

You don't care: you have to have it, please can you have it, please.

On Christmas Day, your oldest sister gets Snow White, and the middle one Aurora, and the youngest Tinkerbell. You open yours, and you see the green felt, and you feel your body turn to stone, to ice, as if you're one of the statues that Polly and Digory from *The Magician's Nephew* find in the cursed hall of the enchanted palace. Your mum has been reading you and your next-oldest sister that book at bedtime, and it gives you nightmares, the thought of all the people trapped inside bodies that are theirs and not-theirs, bodies they can't control or even move, victims of some wicked spell.

And as your dad pulls your pyjama top over your head and manoeuvres your arms into the tunic and buckles the belt and says, Say cheese for the camera!, the feeling intensifies: your body is wrong, and you feel wrong in it.

★

Other things: crying when you have to have your hair cut. Feeling hot and strange and ashamed and confused when everyone laughs at May McFettridge in the Grand Opera House Christmas pantomime. Scribbling your name in febrile secret bursts and adding 'y' and 'ie' and 'ina', trying to find a way of making it sound right. Ripping the pages into tiny scraps afterwards and flushing them down the loo so nobody sees them.

He's just sensitive, your mum says. He's too bloody sensitive, says your dad. And no wonder, this house is like living in a witches' coven.

Your dad gets tickets for a football match, to see Northern Ireland play in the World Cup qualifiers at Windsor Park, but it's your next-oldest sister who begs and begs to go along with him, and in the end he sighs and agrees. At school, like the other boys, you say you hate girls. Girls whisper and they giggle and they're always linking arms and having silly secrets. But at home you sit on your sisters' floors while they paint their nails and practise liquid eyeliner on each other and try on shoes with different outfits and read problem pages out loud in silly voices, and you press yourself as small as you can against the ruffles of their Laura Ashley bedspreads because most of the time when they notice you're there, especially when they're reading the problem pages, they kick you out and you have to sit alone in your room instead.

They used to dress you up too, sometimes, squirt White Musk or Dewberry on you and tell you to pout your lips as they slicked on strawberry-flavoured lipgloss, but as you get older they do that less and less, and after you leave primary school they don't do it at all.

You have dreams where you ache, in places deeper than you can reach. You realise one morning in the shower you have five curling hairs in your groin – you count them, with horror – that seem to have sprouted from nowhere, overnight. You scramble up onto the rim of the bathtub and, balancing there, in front of the mirror, you stare at your body. There are hairs in your armpits, too; three in one, two in another. With clumsy, stabbing fingers, you yank them out using your oldest sister's tweezers, your eyes watering with the pain, but in the following days and weeks they come back faster than you can pluck them out. Your balls itch at night and feel heavy in the mornings when you stand up. You're still small for your age, but your growth spurt will come – your mum tells you, thinking she's being reassuring – and you dread it. You have a hot, sickening feeling that time is running out.

Your house is rarely empty, but one Wednesday evening, it suddenly is. Two of your sisters are in the school play and are still at dress rehearsals; the other is at a friend's house. Your dad is out with clients from work, your mum's going to the Ulster to take flowers to a neighbour who had a bad fall. She asks if you want to come with her, and you say no, and you feel your heart pounding as you realise what this means. You're sure your mum will notice something, realise, insist you come. But she just says, All right, and, Will you be okay on your own? and, Your sisters will be back soon anyway. You watch her car pull out of the driveway, and your heart's in your throat, you can feel it beating there, as if it's lurched up from your chest and lodged there right where the windpipe is.

Then you're turning, pelting up the stairs two or three at a time and standing in the doorway to your sisters' room, the one the eldest two share because there's only a year between them. Their room smells of coconut body balm and Elnett hairspray and ylang-ylang incense sticks. It smells of the jasmine oil that they dab on their wrists and throat and of Clinique Happy, which they mist in the air and step through. It smells of hair singed by GHDs and faintly musty underwear rolled inside out in corners.

You've never been in here alone before. You stand on the threshold, breathing it in. For a moment you even close your eyes. Then the thought that they might be back any moment spurs you on, and you step into the room, picking your way through glittery pools of halter-neck tops and discarded *More!* magazines, frothy concoctions of bras with ribbons for straps and empty Haribo packets. The wardrobe they acrimoniously share is open, bulging: it, like the room, is almost pulsing, bursting with sheer essence of girl.

You know what you're looking for. You root through the wardrobe, heaving overburdened hangers aside, dresses hung higgledy-piggledy, two and three thick. You're look-ing for the dress your oldest sister wore to the Christmas pre-formal last year. It's made from a stretchy gold mater-ial, which you remember is called lamé. Gold lamé: the words are like a spell. The dress is simply cut, straight across the top with tiny straps that are called spaghetti straps. You know this from your sisters' and your mum's discussions and deliberations. It goes right to the floor, and she needed special seamless flesh-coloured underwear with it because the fabric's so thin, or else (your sisters were in fits of gig-gles) she'd have to go commando. You haven't been able to stop thinking about that dress since you first saw it. It stirred something in you.

You find it, eventually, not even in a special bag, just folded over a hanger under a pair of black trousers. Your palms are sweaty now so you wipe them on your jeans before you touch it, then tug it gently from the hanger, shake it out. It's creased, and there's a cigarette burn in it, and a dark spattered stain at the bottom where something has spilt on it, but to you it looks perfect. You open the wardrobe door fully, hold the dress up against yourself and gaze at the mirror inside. Then before you know what you're doing, you're stripping off, shucking off your jeans and pulling off your hoodie and T-shirt, taking each sock off with the heel of the other foot. You stand in your Y-fronts for a moment before yanking them off too.

Your body is pale and hunched, turned in on itself. You're the ugliest sight you've ever seen. But the dress is cool and slippery against your skin. It goes right over your head and falls like a waterfall to your feet, puddling on the floor around you. It gapes at the front, showing your nipples, and one of the straps keeps falling off your shoulder. You need to clutch up a handful of fabric at the side and hold onto the strap with the other hand just to keep it on. But there you are: like a princess.

You lift your chin, pull your shoulders back. If you squint, your hair could be purposefully cropped. There's a word for it, you can't remember the word, but girls have started to do it on purpose. Two of your middle sister's friends did, after Victoria Beckham's wedding last year. You stand on your tiptoes and twist around to see your back, the way the dress ripples when you move.

A sudden flash comes to you of the Belle dress, from all those years ago, and you realise it's the memory you've been reaching for, the thing that hovers at the edge of your dreams, and everything, all at once, makes a terrifying, intoxicating sort of sense.

Look at yourself in that mirror, in that dress. Don't worry about your sisters coming back, or your mum: they won't be home for almost an hour. There's time. Stay where you are, and twist this way and that on your tiptoes, and let your shoulders relax and the knot in your stomach loosen. Look at yourself: how right you look, how beautiful, and remember how it feels, to feel this right, to know you're beautiful.

You don't know it now, but it's a blessing that the mirror can't — like the mirrors in fairy tales — show you what lies ahead. The three long miserable years before you pluck up the courage to say anything. The tubes and tubes of Immac, bought secretly with your pocket money and hidden in amongst your sisters'; that sickening chemical peachy smell, burning your face where you use it too often and leave it on too long. The shame of your voice scratching and hoarsening, the despair of your feet growing too large for your sisters' shoes. The bullying, and the endless beatings-up, no matter how careful you are not to give anything away, because other boys can tell you're different. The nights you cry yourself to sleep. The GP, who will insist there is no service anywhere in Northern Ireland that can help you.

You'll find a website, one day, which will tell you different, which will direct you to forums, statistics, FAQs you can print out. 'How to Tell Your Parents'; 'How to Ask for Help from Your Doctor'. But even after the eventual Tavistock referral will come the endless assessments, the psychologists, the endocrinologists, the journeys to and from Heathrow on the rattling Tube.

And, cruelly, worst of all will be the day you get the go-ahead: your mum trying to speak and for the first time finding nothing to say; your father trying to hug you, to tell you he loves you whatever happens, whatever you decide, his eyes slipping sideways, his voice thick and blurred; your sisters wide-eyed and whispery, flicking each other looks out of the corners of their eyes.

But hold this image of yourself in the gold dress, in front of the wardrobe, in your mind's eye: because you'll need it; and because it will become a sort of talisman; and because no matter what it takes and no matter how long it takes, you will come through.

Here We Are

THE SUMMER IS A WASHOUT. Every day the heavens open, and the rain comes down; not the usual summer showers with their skittish, shivering drops but heavy, dull, persistent rain; true *dreich* days. The sky is low and grey, and the ground is waterlogged, the air cold and damp, blustery.

We don't care. It is the best summer of our lives.

We go to Cutters Wharf in the evenings because nobody we know goes there. It's an older crowd, suits and secretaries, some students from Queen's. Usually we sit inside, but one evening when the clouds lift and the rain ceases, we take our drinks out onto the terrace. The riverfront benches and tables are damp and cold, but we put plastic bags down and sit on those. It isn't warm, but there is the feeling of sitting under the full sky, that pale high light of a Northern evening, and there is the salt freshness of the breeze coming up the Lagan from the lough.

After we leave Cutters Wharf that night, we walk. We walk along the Lagan and through the Holylands: Palestine Street, Jerusalem Street, Damascus Street, Cairo Street. We cross the river and walk the whole sweep of the Ormeau

Embankment. The tide is turning, and a two-person canoe is skimming downriver, slate grey and quicksilver.

When we reach the point where the road curves away from the river, the pale evening light still lingers, so we keep walking, across the Ravenhill Road, down Toronto Street and London Street and the London Road, Rosebery Road and Willowfield Drive and across the Woodstock Road and on, further and further east until we are in Van Morrison territory: Hyndford Street and Abetta Parade, Grand Parade, the North Road, Orangefield.

There are times in your life, or maybe just the one time, when you find yourself in the right place, the only place you could possibly be, and with the only person.

She feels it too. She turns to me. 'These streets are ours,' she says.

'Yes,' I say. 'Yes, they are.' And they were. The whole city was.

★

She was a celebrity in our school, in the way that some girls are. She was the star musician and always played solos at school concerts and prize days and when a minor royal came to open the new sports hall. One year in the talent contest she played the saxophone while another girl sang 'Misty'. They didn't win – some sixth-formers who'd choreographed their own version of 'Vogue' got more votes – but they were the act you remembered. She wore a white suit and sunglasses, but it wasn't that: it was the way she bent over her instrument and swayed, as if it was the most private moment in the world.

It was a few weeks later that her mother was killed. She was out jogging when a carful of teenage joyriders lost control and careened up onto the kerb. They didn't stop: if they had stopped, or at least stopped long enough to ring an ambulance, she might have survived. As it was, she died of massive internal haemorrhaging on a leafy street in Cherryvalley, less than a hundred metres from her home. Her husband was a local councillor and so it made the headlines: the petite blonde jogger and the teenage delinquents.

Her entire class went to the funeral, and the older members of the orchestra, too. I was only a second year and had never even spoken to her, so I just signed the card that went round. She didn't come to practice for several weeks, and there were rumours that she had given up music for good. You'd look for her in the corridors, her face pale and thin with violet bruises under the eyes.

Then, one day, she was there again, sitting in her usual place, assembling her clarinet, and if the teacher was surprised or pleased to see her he didn't let on, and none of the rest of us did either.

She smiled at me sometimes in orchestra practice, but I knew she didn't know who I was. I was two years below, for a start, and she had no way of knowing my name because the music teacher called all three of us flutes 'Flutes'. She smiled because he would make silly mistakes, telling us to go from the wrong place or getting the tempo wrong, and there'd be exaggerated confusion in the screeching, bored, lumbering ranks while he flustered and pleaded and tried to marshal a new start. People were cruel to him, sometimes even to his face. She never was: she just smiled, and because of the way the music stands were laid out I happened to be in the direction of the smile.

I used to say her name to myself sometimes. Angie. Angela Beattie.

What else? She cut her own hair – at least that's what people said, and it looked as if it could be true, slightly hacked at, although the mussed-up style made it hard to tell. Her father was a born-again Christian – he belonged to a Baptist church that spent summers digging wells in Uganda or building schools in Sierra Leone – and when our school joined up with another in West Belfast to play a concert at St Anne's Cathedral she wasn't allowed to take part because it was a Sunday, even though it would be in a church, even though it was for peace.

There was so little I knew about her then.

In the summer term of fourth year, everyone took up smoking, or pretended to. The school was strange and empty that time of year, the Upper Sixth and Fifth Form on study leave, the Lower Sixth promoted to prefects and enjoying their new privilege of leaving the grounds at lunchtime. It was ours to colonise. We linked arms and ducked behind the overgrown buddleia into the alley behind the sports hall, boasting that we needed a smoke so badly we didn't even care if anyone caught us.

The day they did, it was raining and so we weren't expecting it, but all of a sudden there they were, coming down the alleyway, one at each end. I was holding one of the half-smoked cigarettes, and I froze, even as all the others were hissing at me to chuck it away.

The prefect walking towards me was Angie.

I could feel the flurry as those with cigarettes or a lighter scrambled to hide them and others tore open sticks of chewing gum or pulled scarves up around their faces, but only vaguely, as if it was all happening a very long way away.

Angie stopped a couple of metres away. My hand was trembling now. 'Oh my God,' I heard, and, 'What are you at?' and, 'Put it out, for fuck's sake.' But I couldn't seem to move.

Angie looked at me. The expression in her eyes was almost amused. Then, ignoring the nervous giggles and whispered bravado of the others, she took a step forward and reached out for the cigarette. Her fingers grazed mine as they took it from me. She held it for a moment then let it fall to the ground, crushed it with her heel. She looked me in the eye the whole time. I felt heat surge to my face. 'You don't smoke,' she said, and then she said my name.

I felt the shock of it on my own lips. I hadn't known she knew it: knew who I was. She gazed at me for a moment longer in that steady, amused, half-ironic way. Then she said to the other prefect, 'Come on,' and the second girl shouldered past, and they walked back the way Angie had come.

'It's not cool, girls,' she called, without turning round. 'You think it is, but it's not.'

There was silence until they'd turned the corner. Then it erupted: 'What the fuck,' and, 'Oh my God,' and, 'Do you think she's going to report us?', and, 'I am so dead if they do,' and, 'What is she like?', and then, 'Do you reckon she fancies you?' It was the standard slag in our school, but out of nowhere I felt my whole body fizz, felt the words rush through me, through and to unexpected parts of me, the skin tightening under my fingernails and at the backs of my knees.

'Wise up,' I made my voice say, and I elbowed and jostled back. 'It's because of the music. My lungs will be wrecked if I carry on smoking. I actually should think about giving up,' and because we were always talking about having to give up, the conversation turned, and that got me off the hook, at least for the moment.

For the rest of term, I agonised over whether to stop hanging out with the smokers at lunch or whether to keep doing it in case she came back. In the end, I compromised by going behind the sports hall as usual but not inhaling so I could say with all honesty, if she asked, that I didn't smoke any more.

My days became centred around those ten minutes at lunchtime when I might see her again. I would feel it building in me in the last period before lunch, feel my heart start to flutter and my palms become sweaty. But she didn't raid the alleyway again. There was nowhere else I could count on seeing her: orchestra practice had ceased in the last weeks of the summer term – the Assembly Hall was used for examinations and there were too many pupils on study leave anyway – and the sixth-form wing, with their common room and study hall, were out of bounds to fourth-years.

I passed her in the corridor once, but she was deep in conversation with another girl and didn't notice me. On the last day of term, I saw her getting into a car with a group of others and accelerating down the drive, and that was that.

The summer holidays that followed were long. My father, a builder, had hurt his back a few months earlier and had been unable to work so money was tight: there wasn't even to be a weekend in Donegal or a day trip to Ballycastle. The city, meanwhile, battened down its hatches, and I was forbidden to go into town – forbidden, in fact, from going further than a couple of streets away from our house. All my friends who lived nearby were away; I was too old to ride my bike up and down the street or play skipping games like my younger sister.

'Why don't you practise your flute?' my mother would say as I sloped endlessly about the kitchen. Normally I'd roll my eyes, but as the days stretched on I found myself doing it. I didn't admit to myself it was because of Angie Beattie, but as I practised I couldn't help thinking of her. When you first learn the flute, you're told to imagine you're kissing it. Now, every time I put my mouth to the lip plate, I thought of her. I'd think of her mouth, the curve of it. I'd think of the times I'd watched her at the start of orchestra practice, how she'd wet the reed of her clarinet and screw it into place, test it, adjust it, curl and recurl her lips around the mouthpiece. I'd let my mind unfurl, and soon I'd think other things too, things that weren't quite thoughts but sensations, things I didn't dare think in words and that afterwards left me hot and breathless and almost ashamed.

I got good at the flute that summer. When school started up again, the music teacher noticed. He kept me back after the auditions and found me some sheet music, asked me to learn it for the Christmas concert. Then he said he'd had a better idea and rummaged in his desk some more. A sonata for flute and piano, he said – we were short on duets. Angie Beattie could accompany me.

'She might not want to,' I said.

'Nonsense,' he said.

I don't remember much about the first few lunchtime practice sessions we had together. Each one, before it happened, seemed to loom, so inflated in my mind I almost couldn't bear it, then, when it was happening, rushed by. At first I could barely meet Angie's eye: it was mortifying, the extent to which I'd thought about her, let myself daydream about her, and more. But the music was difficult – for me, at least, which made it hard work for her as my accompanist – and that meant there was no time to waste; we needed to get straight to work. After the first week I found I was able to put aside, at least when I was actually with her, the memory of the strange summer's fantasies. But sometimes, late at night, I'd be consumed for an instant with an ache that seemed too big for my body to contain.

One evening, we stayed late practising after school, and, completely out of the blue, she invited me back to her house for dinner. My heart started pounding as I tried to say a nonchalant yes. I'd imagined her house, the rooms she lived in, so many times; I'd imagined so often a scenario in which she might ask me back there. I phoned my mum from the payphone in the foyer, and then we walked back together, down the sweep of the school's long drive, through the drifts of horse chestnut and sycamore leaves in the streets, swinging our instrument cases. There was mist in the air, and, as we turned off the main road, the taste of woodsmoke from a bonfire in a nearby garden.

The Cherryvalley streets were wide and quiet, thick with dark foliage, lined with tall, spreading lime trees. It was all a world away from my street, its neat brick terraces and toy squares of lawn, the gnomes and mini-waterfall in our neighbour's garden that I used to love and show off to schoolfriends before I realised they weren't something to be proud about. Cherryvalley seemed to belong to somewhere else entirely – a different place, or time.

'It's nice around here,' I said.

She glanced at me. 'D'you think so?' There was something in her expression I couldn't read, and I remembered – of course, too late – that her mother had died here, maybe on this very street, or the one we just walked down. The streets felt not quiet but ominous then, the shifting shadows of the leaves, the plaited branches.

'I meant,' I said, flustered, 'the streets have such pretty names.'

She didn't reply, and I tried to think of something else to say, something that would show I was sorry, that I understood. But of course I didn't understand, at all.

We walked on in silence. I wondered what had made her ask me back and if she was already regretting it.

The Beatties' house was draughty and dark. Angie walked through, flipping on light switches and drawing the curtains. I thought of my house, the radio or the TV or often both on at the same time, my mum busy cooking, the cat always underfoot.

Angie made me sit at the kitchen table, like a guest, while she hung my blazer in the cloakroom and made me a glass of lime cordial, then hurried about getting dinner ready. She turned on the oven and took chicken Kievs from the freezer, lined a baking tray with tinfoil, boiled the kettle to cook some potatoes, washed lettuce in a salad spinner and chopped it into ribbons. I had never, I realised, imagined how her home life actually worked. I felt shy of this Angie — felt the two years, and everything else, between us.

When Mr Beattie got back, he looked nothing like the man you used to see shouting on TV or gazing down from lamp-posts. He was tall and thin and washed-out-looking; his shoulders were stooped, and his hair needed cutting. He shook my hand, and I found myself blurting out, 'My dad used to vote for you.' It was a lie: my dad never bothered to vote, and my mum, even though Dad teased her about it, only ever voted Women's Coalition.

I felt Angie looking at me, and I felt my neck and face burning. 'Good man,' Mr Beattie said. 'Every vote counts. These are historic times we're living through.'

'And history will judge us,' I heard myself say. I have no idea where it came from. The car radio, probably, the talk show Mum always had on and always turned off. Mr Beattie blinked, and Angie burst out laughing.

'Indeed,' he said. 'Indeed.'

'He likes you,' Angie said, when Mr Beattie had left the room. 'He really likes you.'

I wasn't sure what there had been to like, but before I could say anything, she said, 'If he talks about church, don't say you don't go.'

'Okay,' I said. 'Why not?'

'Oh,' she said. 'It's just more trouble than it's worth.'

When everything was ready and the three of us sat down at the table, Mr Beattie bowed his head and clasped his hands and intoned a long grace. I looked at Angie halfway through, but she had her head bowed and her eyes closed too. I took care to chime in my 'Amen' with theirs.

As we ate, Mr Beattie asked questions about school, about music. Often Angie would jump in with an answer before I had a chance, and I couldn't work out if it was for my benefit or her father's. When he asked what church I went to, Angie said, 'She goes to St Mark's, don't you?'

'St Mark's Dundela,' Mr Beattie said.

'That's right,' Angie said.

'That's the one,' I said. St Mark's was where our school had its Christmas carol service, the only time of year my family ever set foot in a church, and only then because I was in the choir.

'Good, good,' Mr Beattie said, and I made myself hold his gaze. All that nonsense was just hocus-pocus, is what my dad liked saying. Once, when some Jehovah's Witnesses knocked on our front door and asked if he'd found Jesus, my dad clapped his forehead and said, 'I have indeed, down the back of the sofa, would you believe?' My sister and I had thought it was the funniest thing ever.

'St Mark's Dundela,' Mr Beattie said again. I started to panic then, trying to remember something, anything about it. But he didn't ask any more. 'C. S. Lewis's church,' was all he said, and I smiled and agreed.

The meal seemed to go on for ever. The St Mark's lie had made me feel like a fraud, but it wasn't just that: the whole situation was putting me on edge. Angie was more nervous than I'd ever seen her. In fact, I couldn't think of a time when I had seen her nervous, not when she confronted the smokers, not even before a solo. *I must be doing everything wrong*, I thought. I had the horrible feeling, too, that Mr Beattie could see through me, or, worse, could see into me, into some of the things I'd thought about his daughter.

For dessert there was a chocolate fudge cake, from Marks & Spencer, shiny and dense with masses of chocolate shavings on top.

'Dad has a sweet tooth, don't you, Dad?' Angie said. She cut him a slab of cake, and they grinned at each other for a moment. 'We used to have chocolate cake for dinner sometimes, didn't we?' she said. 'Or cheesecake.'

'Strawberry cheesecake,' Mr Beattie said.

'We reckoned,' she said, turning to me, 'that because it had cheese in it was actually quite nutritious.'

'A meal in a slice,' Mr Beattie said.

'Protein, fat, carbohydrate and fruit,' she said, turning back to him.

'A perfectly balanced plate,' he said, and they smiled that smile again, intimate, impenetrable.

When the meal was finally over, Mr Beattie said, 'Well, after all this talk of the duet, you must give me a concert.'

Without looking at me, Angie said, 'Another time, Dad, we're both played out today,' and I knew she was embarrassed of me. I felt tears boil up in my eyes, and I stood up and said I needed the toilet. I took as long as I could in there, soaping and rinsing my hands several times over, drying each finger. I'd say I had homework, I decided. I'd say my mum didn't like me being out after dark. Both of these things, I told myself, were true.

When I told Angie that I had to go, she looked at me, then looked away. 'Oh,' she said. 'Right.'

Mr Beattie brought my blazer from the cloakroom and said he'd see me to the door. 'It's nice to see Angie bringing a friend back,' he said. 'I look forward to hearing this duet of yours one of these days.'

The whole way home, I felt a strange, fierce sense of grief, as if I'd lost something — a possibility, something that wouldn't come again.

After that, I avoided her, concert or no concert. I went with the smokers at lunch, half-daring her to come and find me, half-dreading it. Thursday and Friday passed without my seeing her. An awful weekend, then Monday and Tuesday, and on Tuesday afternoon I knew I had to skip orchestra practice. On Wednesday she came to the mobile where my class did French, in the middle of a lesson, and said to the teacher she needed to speak to me. She was a prefect, and it was known that we were both musical; the teacher agreed without any questions.

The shock and relief and shame of seeing her coursed through me, and I had to hold onto the desk for a moment as I stood up. As I followed her out of the classroom and down the steps and around the side of the mobile, I couldn't seem to breathe. 'How long are you planning on keeping this up?' she said.

'I don't know,' I said. I could see her pulse jumping in the soft part of her neck. A horrible, treacherous part of me wanted to reach out and touch it.

'Angie,' I said, and from all of the things that were whirling in my head I tried to find the right one to say.

The trees and glossy pressing shrubs around us were thrumming with rain. All the blood in my body was thrumming.

'Look at me,' she said, and, when I finally did, she leaned

in and kissed me. It was brief, only barely a kiss, her lips just grazing mine. Then she stepped back, and I took a step back too and stumbled against the roughcast wall of the mobile. She put out a quick hand to steady me, then stopped.

'Oh God, am I wrong?' she said. 'I'm not wrong, am I?'

Two weeks later, in my house this time, a Saturday night, my parents at a dinner party, my sister at a sleepover. In the living room, in front of the electric fire, we unbuttoned each other's shirts and unhooked the clasps of each other's bras. Then our jeans and knickers: unzipping, wriggling, hopping out and off. We kept giggling – there we were gallivanting around in my parents' living room in nothing but our socks.

'Here we are,' she said, as we faced each other, and my whole body rushed with goosebumps.

'Are you cold?' she said, but I wasn't. It wasn't that, at all.

Afterwards, we pulled the cushions off the sofa and lay on the floor, side by side. After a while we did start to shiver, even with the electric fire turned up fully, but neither of us reached for our clothes, scattered all over like useless, preposterous skins.

'We're like selkies,' she said, 'like *Rusalka* – do you know the opera?' and when I said I didn't, she stood up and struck a pose and sang the water nymph's song to the moon, she told me later, and I jumped to my feet and applauded, and we started giggling again, ridiculous bubbles of joy.

'Here we are,' she said again, and I said, 'Here we are,' and that became our saying, our shorthand. Here we are.

★

All love stories are the same story: the moment that, that moment when, the moment we.

We were we through Christmas, and into the spring. It was so easy: the music had been the reason, and now it was our excuse. We used one of the practice rooms each lunch-time and sometimes after school, and no one questioned it. Sometimes we'd play, or she'd play and I'd listen, or we'd both listen to music, and sometimes we'd just eat our sandwiches and talk. I'd go to hers after school, although I never quite felt at ease there, and I preferred it when we'd go for drives in her car, up the Craigantlet hills or along the coast to Holywood. I drifted from my friends, and she from hers, but the music practice hid everything.

And then we had the summer and we were freer than ever, completely free, and I lied blithely to my parents about where I was going and who with, using a rotating cast of old friends, and neither of them ever cottoned on, and I assumed it was the same for Mr Beattie too.

I don't want to think about the rest of it: the evening he finally confronted us, walked right in on us. I don't want to give any room to the disgust or the revulsion, to the anger and the panic that followed, and the tears, our tears, our wild apologies, when we should have been defiant, because what was there, in truth, for us to be apologising for, and to whom did we owe any apology?

'I have to do it,' she kept on saying. 'I'm all he's got. It won't change anything. But I have to do it.'

★

That winter, my English class studied Keats. I wrote a whole essay, six, seven sides, on the final stanza of 'The Eve of St Agnes'. 'And they are gone: aye, ages long ago / These lovers fled away into the storm.' In the stanza before, the lovers are gliding like phantoms into the wide cold hall and the iron porch where the Porter lies in a drunken stupor. His bloodhound wakes and shakes its flabby face but doesn't bark. The bolts slide open one by one, the chains stay silent, and the key finally turns, then, just as they think they've made it, the door groans on its hinges. You think it's all over for them, but then you read on, and you realise they've slipped away, out of your hands, before your very eyes, a miracle, a magic trick, a wormhole to another place, another time, where no one can ever follow.

The teacher kept me after class. She didn't believe I'd written it, at least not alone. I opened my lever arch and showed her my notes. Page after page after page in my crabbed, self-conscious writing. Ending rights the focus, I'd written, does not leave us in too cosy a glow but reminds us of age/decay/coldness of religious characters. I left this part out: I finished my essay with the lovers escaping. We talked about the real ending, Keats's ending, and we talked about his drafts of the ending, some of which were printed in the footnotes of the cheap Wordsworth edition.

'You've really thought about this,' she said. 'You've really taken this to heart.' I started to cry. 'Oh dear,' the teacher said, and she found me a tissue from a plastic pouch in her desk drawer, and she came round and sat on the front of her desk and asked if there was anything I wanted to talk about. I shook my head and held out my hand for my essay, and I wondered how much she knew, or guessed, my whole body liquid with shame.

★

I looked her up on the Internet just once, some months ago, on impulse, spurred by the Marriage Equality march in Belfast. It instantly felt too easy, too much. She'd never made it as a solo or even an orchestral musician, but she was a music teacher – and she was married; she and her husband ran a small music school together in Ayrshire. There were pictures of them both on the website, taking group lessons, conducting ensembles, standing with students of the most recent Woodwind Summer School. She was still whippet thin, no make-up, choppy hair. He looked younger than her: Doc Martens and skinny jeans, spiky hair, an earring. I clicked from one picture to the next. I don't know why I was so taken aback. I was engaged, after all. Engaged, happily engaged, and about to buy a flat. I just had never imagined it for her.

A memory came to me: one time in Ruby Tuesday's, or The Other Place, one of the studenty cafés across town in South Belfast where you could sit and eke out a mug of filter coffee for a whole evening. We'd said I love you by then – maybe for the first time, or maybe very recently; we were huge and important and giddy with it, with all of it, with us. I felt as if my blood was singing – that sparks were shooting from me – that everything I touched was glowing.

I could have done anything in those weeks. I could have run marathons or swum the length of the Lagan or jumped from a trapeze and flown. And yet I was happy, happier than I thought it was possible to be, just sitting in a café, talking. We sat in that café and talked about everything and nothing, talked and talked, and we were us. I remember that; I couldn't get over that. The room and everything in it: the scuffed wooden booths, the chipped laminate tables, the oversized menus, the fat boys in Metallica T-shirts and Vans at the table beside us, the cluster of girls across the way still in their school uniforms, the waitress carrying a plate of profiteroles, the rain on the window, the yellow of the light – it seemed a stage set that had been waiting our whole lives for us and at last we were here.

The waitress at the table, splashing more coffee into our mugs: 'Anything else I can get for yous, girls?' and we say, 'No, thank you,' in unison, then burst out laughing, at nothing, at all of it. For all the waitress knows, for all anyone knows, we're just two students, two friends, having an ordinary coffee.

'I want to tell her,' I say. 'I want to stand up and tell everyone.' And for a moment it seemed as if it might just be that simple: that that was the secret. 'I don't want us to have to hide,' I went on. 'I want to tell everyone: my parents, your dad, everyone. I want to stand in front of the City Hall with a megaphone and shout it out to the whole of Belfast.'

Suddenly neither of us was laughing any more.

'I wish we could,' she said.

We were both quiet for a moment.

'When you were older,' I said, thinking aloud, 'you could team up with a male couple, and the four of you could go out together, and people would assume, assume correctly, you were on a double-date. Only the couples wouldn't be what they thought.'

I was pleased with the idea, but she still didn't smile. 'Hiding in plain sight,' she said.

'You could live together,' I went on, 'all in one big house, so your parents wouldn't get suspicious. If you had to, you could even marry.' I started laughing again as I said it.

'No,' she said, and she was serious, more than serious – solemn. She reached out and touched one finger to my wrist and all of my blood leapt towards her again. 'We won't need to,' she said. 'By then we'll be free.'

That night, I walked the streets of East Belfast again in my dreams. Waking, the dream seemed to linger far longer than a mere dream. *These streets are ours.* I was jittery all day, a restless, nauseous, over-caffeinated feeling. I could email her, I thought, through the website. I wouldn't bother with pleasantries or preliminaries, I'd just say, 'There we were. Do you remember?'

Chasing

I STEPPED INTO THE PORCH AND HAULED my suitcases in behind me.

'Close the outer door before you open the inner one, remember,' Mum said. 'The plants don't like the draught.' Then she went to park the car round the back. I bumped the front door shut with my hip. There seemed to be more plants than ever. The succulents, the geraniums, the spineless yucca. A spider fern in a hanging basket was shooting out runners and making clumps of babies in a desperate attempt to reach the floor. I managed to get my bags and myself through the pot plants without knocking any over and opened the inner door to the hallway.

The house smelt clean and still. Mum had steamed the curtains with the Polti and polished the parquet tiles for my arrival. I stood, looking around. The pine cones in their bowl in the fireplace, which would be replaced in December with gold ones she'd spray-paint herself. My sister's and my profiles, cut from sugar paper by a street artist in Paris all those years ago, carefully transported and mounted and framed.

I heard Mum coming in the back door, putting down her handbag and keys, taking off her shoes and coat. I hadn't taken off my own shoes yet. For some reason, I couldn't seem to move. 'The house looks lovely,' I called out. 'So clean.' My voice sounded too loud, forced.

'Right,' Mum said, coming down the corridor. 'Let's get your things upstairs then.'

'Great,' I said.

It was harder with two people than it would have been with one, manoeuvring each bag around the dog-leg landing, Mum at one end, me at the other. Down the landing, a step at a time. The carpet in my old room had been freshly steam-cleaned too, and there were yellow and pink carnations in a vase on the window sill.

'There you are,' Mum said.

'It looks lovely,' I said again.

'I'll put the kettle on,' Mum said. 'Come down when you're ready.'

I was ashamed, suddenly, of the long, gulping, incoherent phone conversations. We wouldn't mention them again: I knew that.

There wasn't enough room in the wardrobe for me to hang my things. My dad had started keeping his winter overcoats and bulkier suits in there, and the rest was taken up with my jotters and lever-arch files, going all the way back through secondary school. I didn't know why I'd kept them. The Weimar Republic, Metternich, the Russian Revolution. I'd known this. It seemed improbable now. Earlier files were graffitied with the slogans of Therapy? and The Levellers, bands I'd copied from our babysitter, pretended to love.

I was still looking through the files when Mum called up that she had to collect Molly from school then take her to her music lesson. My cup of tea was on the kitchen counter, she said, though I might want to put it in the microwave for thirty seconds. I listened to the back door closing, the car starting up and reversing down the drive, pausing at the gate and moving off. I had forgotten how suburban silence felt. The click of the central heating kicking in. The quarterly ting of the hallway clock.

I got up and went downstairs. The tea was barely even lukewarm. I poured it down the sink, rinsed out the mug and put it upside down in the draining rack. The window by the sink looked out onto the neighbours' new fence, six feet high, the yellow wood still raw-looking, and my parents' army of bins: blue for recycling, brown for compostable, black for all other waste.

With a rush of relief I decided to get rid of some of my old stuff. I found a roll of heavy-duty waste sacks in the utility room and went back upstairs. But I overfilled them: as soon as I tried to lift them, the bottoms broke, and the files tumbled out again. Suddenly tired, I stacked everything back where it had been. My clothes I bundled into drawers and what didn't fit into the drawers I just left in the suitcases, pushed under the bed. Then I lay back on the bed and let myself realise what I knew already, what I'd known almost as soon as I set foot through the door.

Coming back was not the answer.

Molly and Mum were making a terrarium for Molly's GCSE art project. They'd found, in the attic, the huge glass carboy that had sat in Mum's flat in the seventies, and they were filling it with a species of plant called *Tillandsia* that they bought online, an air plant that didn't need soil or even much water. Molly was experimenting too with making miniature terraria out of lightbulbs. She snapped the metal tips off with pliers and yanked the wiring out, then lined each bulb with a teaspoon of sand and a few strands of desiccated moss, finally inserting the baby tillandsia with tweezers. She intended to tie invisible thread around them and hang them from picture hooks on the ceiling, in clusters. The theme of her project was Self-Contained.

She gave me one of the early lightbulbs. There were all sorts of rules about terraria, like bonsai trees or flower-arranging, and she was having fun with them. To mine, along with the sand and the moss and the wisp of fern, she'd added a Lego figure and some small coloured blocks so that it looked as if the Lego person was building her own house in the jungle. She'd decided it was too silly for her final project, but it was impossible to dismantle the bulb without breaking it. I hung it from the paper lampshade in my bedroom, and it twisted and swayed, a fragile bubble of a new world in thrall to its huge implacable sun, or moon.

I got vague back home. Even a few days in I could feel myself blurring. I developed a habit of reading the first chapter or sometimes only the first few pages of the books

I'd loved as a child then finding myself unable to read any more. Or I'd spend a long time choosing a book to read, whole afternoons going through boxes in the attic, then not be able to summon up the energy to start it.

We hadn't discussed how long I'd be back for, and we hadn't discussed what I'd do next. 'You just need a break,' my parents kept on saying. None of us ever said, at least not out loud, that a break can also mean something is broken. This was a good break, a rest, a recuperation. And who knew – my mother was careful to say this only once, and in a deliberately off-hand way – maybe I'd decide I wanted to stay. Things were really picking up here. The new name for the Belmont Road and Ballyhackamore was the Upper East Side, there were that many new cafés and bistros and shops. One morning – it must have been the second or third week back – Mum found me holding an old cassette tape, a collection of songs that had been childhood favourites of ours, and crying.

'Right,' she said, and she bundled me into the car and drove us into town, to Bradbury Graphics, and spent a small fortune buying me new canvases and oils and a book of tear-off palettes. 'Look,' she said, 'isn't this fabulous? You don't have to spend hours scraping the old paint off, you just throw it away and tear out a new one. Isn't that just fabulous?' The assistant was my age and obviously at art school – an undercut, pink-streaked hair – and I didn't meet her eye.

That evening, Dad dug out the spare easel from the garage and set it up for me, on sheets of newspaper in the dining room. By the utility-room sink they lined up a row of jam jars for my brushes and a tub of white spirit. They were trying too hard.

'Thank you,' I said. 'It's really good of you all. Thanks.'

'Only you will remember, won't you,' Mum said, 'not to pour any paint or turpentine down the sink?'

'I was fourteen,' I said.

For a day or two I tried, or pretended to. I primed my own canvas the textbook way, rubbing it down with sandpaper after the first layer of primer had dried, adding a second, then a third. I held it under an anglepoise lamp at all angles to check for clumps or bumps or rough patches, and it was perfect.

Then I decided to put down a coloured ground and squeezed three fat worms of yellow ochre onto my palette and a single worm of titanium white. It was as we'd been taught at A Level, the traditional way of painting. Yellow ochre, toned down with white, is the best beginner's choice because it's brighter than you think and will make you paint more boldly, Ms Donnelly said.

My tutor at art college had snorted with derision when she saw me painting that way. It was timid and old-fashioned, she said; no one painted that way any more. Not since the Impressionists had a real artist laid down a coloured ground. All it did was take away the fear of the blank canvas, and you had to face that fear. She barely commented on my work for the rest of the term. She wasn't that interested in painting, anyway – no one was, even though it was meant to be a fine-art college. They liked conceptual art.

I signed up for a private course of life-painting classes, and the tutor there insisted that you paint straight onto the white as well. They were both right. The colours were utterly different when you painted onto white: brighter, more vibrant. An opaque primed surface reflected back more light too, even under the colours, especially if you were painting with oils. The painting was more alive in every way. For a while it was exhilarating.

I gazed at the canvas, at my palette, picked up my palette knife and blended the paint I'd squeezed, the streaks of white reluctant at first, then giving way, the yellow ochre turning creamy. I stopped. I'd thought that if I could go back to how I'd felt most comfortable, how I'd first learned, it would help, but it didn't. I was just delaying. I tore off the top palette and folded it up; such a waste of paint. Then I sat down at the table instead and watched Molly. She was cutting and gluing and making collages and hasty charcoal drawings, filling a sketchbook with what was meant to be the initial inspiration for her project, the story of its conception. She finished a drawing of an air plant, copied from a webpage on her laptop in front of her. *Tillandsia juncia*, this one was called, tall and slender with hair-like fronds. She'd done it with white charcoal on black paper, not particularly carefully; she tore it from the sketchpad and slid it into her book. 'Ms Donnelly says I've to have at least ten of these,' she said, and rolled her eyes. She had grown up, even in just the few months I'd been away. She sat straighter, talked louder.

'Ms Donnelly,' I said.

'She says I'll get marked down if I can't show where the idea came from. How am I supposed to know where the idea came from?'

'Where did it come from?'

'I don't know. Mum was just sorting some stuff out for the cancer shop and she found the glass thingy. Then we looked them up online.'

Molly started another. I moved to sit beside her and looked at the screen. *Tillandsia ioantha*. The tillandsias looked like shy underwater creatures, spiders or anemones, or like life forms from another planet. Molly drew red tips on the ioantha. 'Are you not painting anything?' she said.

'Sorry,' I said. 'Am I putting you off?'

'It's okay,' she said, and there was a sudden silence. She watched me for a moment. Then she looked away and picked at her lips. She'd had her braces off – she'd had full-on train tracks, top and bottom, elastic bands in between – and she still plucked at where they used to be. 'What happened?' she said, fast. 'I mean – what actually happened?'

'I don't know,' I said, and there was another silence.

'Here,' she said. 'Will you do one for me?'

She ripped out a sheet of black paper and pushed over the box of charcoals so it sat in between us. Then she turned to her laptop and scrolled down the screen. 'I need this one – *magnusiana* – or else you can do this one, *incarnata*.'

'I don't mind,' I said.

'Do both then. I don't need them to be any good, I just need to show I've done them.'

I started on the magnusiana, a thick purple spike and frail silvery leaves. For a while, both of us drew in silence. 'Did I tell you I bumped into Veronica?' I found myself saying.

'Veronica?' Molly said. 'Veronica Moore?'

'Yeah. Veronica Moore.' Veronica had been our babysitter when we were younger, in our old house, when her family lived next door. Sometimes, if she was looking after us during the day, she'd take us to have orange squash and biscuits in her house. We'd watched over the hedge between our front gardens as she'd spray-painted her Doctor Martens purple then had to spray-paint them again a week later, black this time, when her boyfriend said he couldn't stand the colour.

'Where did you bump into her?'

'In a bar, just.'

Molly waited for me to go on. 'And?' she said, when I didn't.

'That's it,' I said, and she rolled her eyes.

'It was funny to see her,' I said.

'Yeah,' Molly said, vaguely.

I couldn't explain how strange it had been to see Veronica Moore, to see her and to think that there was hardly any difference between us now. The handful of years had been a gulf, but it had shrunk, to the extent that we could find ourselves in the same East London bar. It had seemed impossible, somehow – magical.

'Hi,' I'd said, drunk and incredulous. 'Veronica, it's me,' and I'd insisted on dragging her through the crowds to meet my friends. 'This is Veronica,' I'd announced. 'She used to be my babysitter.' A couple of people had greeted her, polite but uninterested, and the others sized her up and dismissed her. I'd felt my face burn for her. 'She used to be my babysitter,' I said again. She was wearing a neat fitted dress and nude court shoes, too much make-up, straightened hair. She looked like a secretary, I realised, and my face burned all over again on my own account. I had tried to think of something more to say and couldn't think of a thing.

'Well,' she'd said eventually, 'I'd better get back to—' and she gestured at the man she was with, flustered now, and I'd wondered if I had interrupted a date.

'Okay!' I'd said, then, not knowing what else to do, blurted out, 'We must swap numbers and meet up!'

She'd blinked. 'Sure,' she'd said, and recited her mobile number to me. 'Right, well. Say hi to your mum from me.'

'I will do!' I'd said. The exclamation marks were too loud at the end of every sentence I spoke, I could hear them.

'She spray-painted her DMs purple once and then had to spray-paint them black because her boyfriend said he couldn't stand the colour purple,' I'd said, to no one in particular, and no one had heard or bothered to reply.

I stood up. I walked across the dining room to the sideboard, where Molly's mail-order tillandsias sat in their sealed plastic bubbles in individual polystyrene blocks. They made you think of moon landings, of other worlds. Cape Canaveral on *Blue Peter*. Of the craze in primary school for astronauts' ice cream in freeze-dried powdery blocks. Molly's project was a good project.

'Are you going to do Art?' I said.

'What do you mean?' she said.

'Like for A Level.'

'Nu-uh. To do biology you need to have Biology, Chemistry, Physics and Maths. It's just to show I'm well rounded.'

'It's a good project,' I said.

She looked at me. We'd been close as children, despite the four years between us, but I'd been awful to her in our teens. I'd banned her from wearing clothes like mine, even from doing her hair like mine. We didn't look alike, not enough that you'd know straight away that we were sisters, and when she started secondary school I'd refused to acknowledge her in the corridors. She'd had buck-teeth and glasses; I'd feared she'd be social death for me.

'Seriously,' I said.

'Thanks,' she said, still wary, still suspecting a trap.

For the rest of that week, I helped Molly with her sketch-book after dinner. I even redid her hasty charcoal drawings for her, copying her style as closely as possible, so Ms Donnelly wouldn't suspect. Then it was finished and there was no more to do. I wandered through to the kitchen where Mum was folding laundry. 'Mum?' I said, leaning my head into her neck.

'Yes, love?' She stopped folding for a moment, stroked a loose strand of hair back from my forehead. Her fingers were dry and calloused. I thought suddenly of the tub of Atrixo on the window sill above the sink when we were growing up, of sinking my own fingers into the greasy cold white cream. The memory was so vivid that for an instant I could smell it. Atrixo, onions and garlic frying, the chill damp air when you pressed your nose up against my father's herringbone overcoat. It all welled up inside me, what I'd done, what I'd lost. My throat ached. 'What is it, sweetheart?' my mother said.

We'd seen the Leah Betts video at school, in Third Form. The youth worker who visited the school to screen it had one ear pierced to show he was cool, but his bad stubble rash and obvious embarrassment at being in an all-girls' school let him down. We sensed his discomfiture and during his introductory talk we were merciless, outdoing each other with scenarios in which people might offer you drugs and saying 'No' would not be possible. The scenarios were outlandish, preposterous. It was nigh-on impossible to get drugs in Belfast then anyway; that's what people said. Thank heavens for small mercies, is what my parents said.

The mood changed when he showed us the video. Even as Leah Betts blew out the birthday candles on her own cake and the camera flashed and clicked to capture it, she only had an hour left to live. 'She said that her head was hurting,' Leah's best friend said, 'and she couldn't feel her legs, and she wanted her mum.' That had been the scariest thing: it had happened in her own home, in her living room, with her family there. The video made a lot of this, showing a still of the peach bathroom sink where Leah Betts had got the water that killed her, then a lingering close-up of the cold tap itself with its acrylic handle, the plug chain slung casually around it. You were never safe. Afterwards, the youth worker Blu-tacked up a poster of her, slack-jawed on a ventilator, already brain-dead, and we all cried and hugged each other and promised him and each other and ourselves that we'd never take drugs. 'Just Say No' was all you had to do. It was like an amulet, a magic spell to keep you safe. So long as you went through life just saying no, no harm could come to you.

There was no reason why I said, 'Can I?'

The first time, I'd just watched, and no one had tried to pressure me. I'd smoked a joint instead, though I didn't like the heavy, nauseous feeling it gave me, and no one laughed or said anything about me being provincial, or conservative, or any of the other things I knew I must seem – was. The next time it was passed round, I just took it. That was the thing: you didn't have to Say No, you didn't even have to say yes, and besides, no one really cared. Can I? Sure. No biggie.

They were smoking it in a bong, a trick someone had read about online, to be more economical: you needed less, and it was stronger. There was no blackened tinfoil or teaspoons and certainly no syringes. They called it 'opium' and had spent the past week talking about Coleridge and Shelley and Thomas De Quincey, about The Velvet Underground.

I took the bulb and clamped my lips around the wet nozzle of the pipe and inhaled. Almost immediately my skin started tingling, then prickling, like pins and needles, and I thought that I might vomit there and then, in front of everyone, all over everyone, and I couldn't stop thinking of Leah Betts. Ten minutes from now she'd be screaming in agony. Within half an hour she'd be dead. She thought she was fine: she was laughing and dancing and enjoying her party, but the clock was ticking for her now, and these were the last minutes, the only minutes, she had left to live.

But the shaky feeling passed, and the next time the vaporiser came round, I took it again, and this time I felt my breathing lengthen and all of the awkward, cumbersome parts of me fall away, as if for years I'd been holding my breath tightly balled in my chest until finally I could let it go, and I thought, *This is it.* A woozy half-hour later, I was loose-limbed and nauseous but fine. I had done it. Heroin. There was a before and after to my life now – something there'd never been before.

It didn't seem to change anything for the rest of them. I couldn't get my head round that at first. For them, I realised, even as we talked about it the following day, it had been an adventure, something to do because we were young and at art school and it was the end-of-term party. There was no reason it should have been any different for me. I couldn't explain what it was, or why it might be. It wasn't that I had any trauma to wipe out. I hadn't had any strange or striking ideas either, like people talked about so longingly, but then I hadn't, anyway, before. It had been a blankness, a sense of afterwards, an atonement for something I didn't even know needed atoning for, and it had been so easy, too easy.

That was the thing that scared me most, in the following days, as I thought and thought about it and couldn't stop thinking about it. Now I had done it once, what was to stop me doing it again, and again, and again? I decided I had to leave art college, and London. Maybe it was over-reacting. Maybe it was just an excuse for something else entirely. But what if it wasn't?

Molly finished her terraria project, and we went to see it at the school's open day. The big terrarium and the cluster of little light bulbs didn't look like they had enough space, in among all of the other GCSE and A-Level art: the photographs of someone's pregnant aunt; the huge, Francis Bacon-inspired canvases of hanging animal carcasses; the dress riveted out of beaten, flattened Coke cans. Someone else won the Art Prize. Molly said it didn't matter. We all, Mum, Dad and me, said she should have won it. I had won it. Molly said it really didn't matter, she wasn't going to do it for A Level, anyway.

Ms Donnelly said hello but deliberately didn't ask how I was or what I was doing. I smiled and said I hadn't liked London, I'd missed home too much, I might reapply for the University of Ulster next year. It came out easily, and it sounded true, or at least as if it could be. I felt my parents not-glancing at each other as I said it, heard every word of their silent conversation of relief. 'Ah, so you're still painting, then,' Ms Donnelly said, and I smiled and nodded, and everyone was too busy not making a big deal out of the University of Ulster to notice the lie.

Back home, I lay on my bed, gazing at the slowly twisting terrarium. For a brief moment, I thought of smashing it, of freeing the Lego Amazon and her handful of bricks from the clutches of the spidery fern. But I thought it might hurt Molly's feelings and so I didn't; I just let it hang there, still turning.

Inextinguishable

THREE DAYS BEFORE MY DAUGHTER DIED she comes running into the kitchen, Mummy, Mummy, you have to listen to this piece of music.

I would have been doing the ironing at the time. Two sons at secondary school and a husband needing a clean shirt every day, there are times when it feels I do nothing but ironing. Even your so-called non-iron fabrics need ironing.

So in she comes, You really have to get hold of it, Mum, and she writes down the name on a piece of paper and sticks it to the fridge. And, needless to say, I immediately forget all about it.

We weren't a classical-music sort of family. Her daddy's tone-deaf, and as for me, I couldn't carry a tune in a bucket with a lid on it. The children did Music in school – recorders and that – but that's about the extent of it. Carols at Christmas. The Wheels on the Bus. My husband likes a bit of Frank Sinatra. But aside from that, the only music we really listened to was on *The X Factor*, or Cool FM when it came through the floorboards of one of the boys' rooms upstairs.

My daughter's interest in music was unexpected, and very new. It started when she got the car. She was so proud of that car, and we were so proud of her. She hadn't really the grades or inclination to go to university, and, besides, she'd her heart set on being a nursery assistant: she loved being around the little ones. Her brothers are five and seven years younger than her, and she just doted on them.

She'd got a place on an early years course, only it was in the city centre, and it would have taken two buses and too long to get in and out each day. So for the whole of the summer after sixth form she worked three jobs to earn enough money to buy her own car. Daytimes she worked at the chemist's, then four nights a week in the hotel bar, and on Sundays she worked at the old people's home. The whole summer long. Her friends were all in Magaluf and that, Tenerife, but she just worked, and she never complained, and we were just so very proud of her.

By the end of August she'd saved up enough, and we gave her £400 towards it too, the insurance and what-have-you, and she bought a cherry-red Citroen Saxo, five years old but hardly anything on the mileage. The only thing was, the radio was banjaxed. It was jammed on a classical station, and when you tried to tune in to CityBeat or Cool FM, all you got was static.

When she told us this, we said that for her birthday we'd buy her an in-car CD player, but she said she actually didn't mind, that she quite liked the classical music in the mornings. The roads are awful in the mornings, worse it seems each year, jam-packed with cars and angry people late for work, and she said it was soothing, that it helped her drive more safely.

Two days before, she says to me, Have you ordered it yet, Mum? And when I said no, she goes, For heaven's sake, Mummy, just log on to Amazon and order yourself a copy, I've the name of the composer and everything written out for you. I promised I would, and I did intend to, but I didn't.

The day before, she logged on to Amazon and clicked and bought it herself. It arrived three days after. Three days . . . after.

★

I'm not going to talk about how she died, and immediately after. I can't think of her like that. I don't want anyone to be left with those images in their head, or even to have the chance to think of her like that.

★

We didn't know what music to play at the funeral, and it didn't even occur to me to look at the CD. In the end, we went for hymns the priest suggested – 'Abide with Me' and 'The Day Thou Gavest Lord Is Ended' – and her school-friends chose one by your woman from The Pogues, her name escapes me, singing Thank you for the days . . .

Back at the house, one of her friends who played the

guitar did a sort of – I suppose you'd call it reggae – version of 'Somewhere Over the Rainbow', and those of us that weren't crying before were broken by the end.

The CD just stayed in a pile, with all the other post that came for her, bank statements and junk mail, clothing catalogues and her magazine subscriptions, none of which I could bear, not even the charity begging letters, to open and throw away. It was at least a few months before I brought myself to deal with it, to go through the stack and contact everyone who had her on their database. And even then I didn't throw away the envelopes, or even the plastic wrapping with her name sticky-labelled onto it, because how could you just throw it in the bin?

When I finally opened the cardboard package and took out the CD, that Tuesday night came back to me, the damp smell of the ironing, a casserole in the oven, the boys fighting upstairs and the radio on with the news, and when she came hurrying in I told her to mind where the finished shirts were piled over the back of the chair, that she didn't knock them off; and I didn't properly listen to her or even ask her why. It would have been so easy to, but I was busy and dinner was going to be late, and her coming in all bursting to tell me was just one more thing adding to the noise and the chaos. Mummy, Mummy, you have to listen to this piece of music. How easy would it have been just to put down the iron for a second and say, Oh really? That sounds interesting, I'm all ears, tell me why.

I'd love to say I got it straight away, but the truth of it is, I didn't. You're sort of straight in with no warning, and it's all clashing drums and sounds like sirens, shrieking strings. I was first of all taken aback then horribly disappointed. It wasn't nice music – it was only noise, demonic discordant noise, and I couldn't for the life of me hear what she'd heard in it, and I wondered if maybe she'd made a mistake. I thought maybe she heard something else entirely, and she misheard the announcer – or the announcer announced a piece that was coming up later – or even the announcer made a mistake – and I wondered was there a way to contact the station and get a list of everything they'd played that afternoon and evening on that date, because I was sure the piece she'd come in raving about could not be this. Yet she'd been so sure, and I'm certain she would have double-checked when she was buying it, listened to the clip on the website, made sure she was getting the right recording. She was like that.

For that reason, I couldn't quite bring myself to turn the music off. So I knelt there for her on the living-room floor, in front of the CD player like I was praying, and listened to the whole thing through, wondering over and over why on earth this, and wanting to cry. When it ended, I played it again, in despair, and I had just tried it for one last time when the boys came crashing in from school. No: not 'crashing', crashing's what they used to do. Those days they tiptoed, or at least tried to. Closed the door properly rather than slamming it. Shoes wiped on the mat and off in the porch, blazers hung up. There were times I wanted to scream at them to hurtle in like they used to, muddy footprints through the hall, coats discarded where they fell,

What's for tea and straight to the fridge to see what they could scrounge and fighting over it. That afternoon they came in quietly, and when I wasn't in the kitchen checked my bedroom, and finally found me there in the front room.

It had got dark since I went in there, and cold, and I was just kneeling on the floor feeling empty. Because, of course, I'd put the CD on hoping desperately for a message, or something, a connection, and feeling nothing was worse than not having tried in the first place, and I was cursing myself for letting myself think there might have been something, for it was like losing her all over again, another part of her I didn't know, until I'd lost it, that I'd lost.

The boys asked me what I was at, and I told them. They asked me to play it again so they could hear. I told them they wouldn't like it, that I'd no idea what to make of it, that I couldn't for the life of me see why their sister had been so insistent. Put the light on then, my elder son said, but I said no because I didn't want them to see how much I'd been crying, because it does something to them, it sort of freezes them up. So we sat there in the dark, and I pressed play once more.

A funny thing happened then.

As soon as it started – didn't the boys just love it? They genuinely thought it was class, according to them it was all space rockets and Martian invasions, *Star Wars* and intergalactic apocalypse. We whacked the volume up to full so the whole room was reverberating, I mean at times you could hear the wedding crystal in the cabinet shivering like it was going to shatter.

And this time – it was probably to do with the boys' reaction to it – the marching bits actually started to make me think of troops off to war. It sounds fanciful now, but for a moment or two I could hear their swords or sabres or what-have-you glinting. Even the slow bits that some-times didn't really have a tune sounded better than they had before. So there we were, sat listening, and occasionally my youngest would leap up and jump around. I hadn't seen him so animated since – well, before. It probably helped we were sat there in the dark, with the music blasting out as loud as the system could manage and the floors buzz-ing when the drums went off, the vibrations going right through our bodies, like we were actually inside the music. It was . . . freeing.

I sound like I'm off my trolley, but that's how it felt. We listened to the whole thing through – I wouldn't have believed it of my sons, over half an hour – and when it ended, in that big euphoric surge, the boys collapsed in a heap and giggling over their battle, it felt like we'd – what would be the word – wrested something back from the chaos and the fury of it all.

I played it to my husband that night, when the boys were in bed. It wasn't the same though: sitting on the sofa with the lights on and the volume respectable. To avoid looking at him, because I could see my watching for a reaction was making him uncomfortable, I took out the sleeve notes – the CD came with a wee booklet of essays. The symphony was written, it said, against the backdrop of the Great War, or what we now know as the First World War – and there were quotes from letters the composer had written to his wife, setting out what he wanted to do, and what he wanted to achieve, some expression of the way life will always triumph, the – 'indomitable' was the word used – will of everything living, be it humans, animals, or even plants, to survive.

My husband didn't really get it, though he nodded and tried to pretend he had, but I just told him, Give it a few more goes. With music like that, with so many layers and stories in it, and huge long passages of what you wouldn't even really consider to be music, you need time and repetition for it to weave its way inside of you.

Listen to you, he said, when I'd finished explaining that to him, and he shuffled across the no-man's land between us on the sofa and put his arm around my shoulders, and I let my head rest on him, and it felt like the first time that we'd touched each other without it being as if one or both of us were clinging to a life raft.

You sometimes wonder if she somehow knew, you know? I mean of course she didn't, but you sometimes wonder.

I don't mean to suggest that everything was suddenly all right then because of course it wasn't . . . isn't. But when I think back to that year and those endless months after, that evening feels in some ways like a turning point, a glimpse of hope.

I've listened to it many times now, that symphony, but whenever I talk about it I still get the name of it wrong; it's a clumsy name, and doesn't come easily. I call it 'Undistinguishable' instead of 'Inextinguishable', and I have to catch myself, in case someone goes searching for it. Though I suppose that's got a meaning in itself, because we're undistinguishable people, we're not rich or famous or anybody really, but the music's for us, too. You think you have to be educated or clever, but you don't.

My youngest son started learning the drums a while back, God help us, inspired by the battle at the end, and we've bought him a drum set on eBay for his sixteenth birthday, though it's going to have to live in the garage.

'Inextinguishable': it's a clumsy word to express something that maybe words can't but that the music can. Something about us all being here – alive – and there being hope, even when there isn't. The whole of life being one big thing, always moving, like a great rushing stream, and us just wee droplets in it.

My elder son's eighteen, now. There are days when I still don't think I can get up in the mornings. But you do. You do because you have to. You do because it's not just you – it's other people, something bigger than you – and this is what the music is too, or what it reminds us.

That's not quite it, and I'm all too aware I can't quite explain what I mean. Sometimes it's not a consolation that life goes on. The opposite. Sometimes I say to myself that music was my daughter's final gift to us, because we listen to it all the time now, we have a whole shelf of classical CDs. Other times, of course, I'd swap every single note of music ever written for one last chance to see her, just five minutes, just one hug. I don't believe in an afterlife, as such, the way the priests describe. Fluffy clouds and harps and your loved ones in eternal spring. But I don't think that we end, either, ever. No matter what life does to you and even after life as we know it is over, I think that something remains that cannot be destroyed or put out. So there we have it, for want of a better word: inextinguishable.

Cyprus Avenue

DECEMBER HAS ALWAYS BEEN HARD, but this year will be the hardest December yet. You will feel yourself struggling to shoulder the weight of it, will want, more keenly than ever, to shrug it off, just this once, just for one year, and you'll find yourself saying on the phone to your mum, I might not actually be able to get home. The last word will stick in your throat, and you'll hear her hear it, feel your heart beating. Your mum will clear her throat and say nothing, wait for you to say, The flights are so booked up, and, My boss . . .

But the excuses you've rehearsed so persuasively in your head will die away on your lips. You'll picture her, standing in the middle of the draughty hallway wearing her padded bodywarmer and scarf because even with the central heating on full blast she feels the cold too much these days, holding her mobile in its bright-pink shellac case, the vacuum, or the laundry, or whatever it was she was doing when you phoned abandoned at her feet. Mum . . . you'll say, and she'll say, Oh it's all right, I understand. And so you will end the call by saying, I'll get on the website now, and you'll hang up the phone and curse your mother, and curse yourself, and you'll end up in the departures lounge on the twenty-third of December as always, waiting for an interminably delayed allegedly budget airline to announce the flight is boarding for Belfast.

The Belfast flight is always shunted to a far corner of the airport, a hangover from when its passengers needed to be corralled, observed. It is an exiles flight: there may be a handful of English or half-English kids visiting their Northern Irish parent's folks for Christmas, but the majority are those who have left for good, all travelling back at the last possible minute, most guilty, some maudlin, few happy.

You will have been delayed for almost three hours by the time the harassed-looking ground staff, in their cheap tunics and flashing Santa hats, will hand out vouchers for food and drinks. You'll have laid your book aside a while ago, and you will have been studying faces, listening. It's strange how quickly your ear tunes back in, how suddenly it's the ground staff's English voices that sound too loud and brash, so sure of themselves and yet so out of place. You've lost your accent, years ago and mostly on purpose, but when you accept the vouchers you'll hear the vowels tightening, the inflections in your voice creeping back. One of you, one of us, one of them.

There's only one bar at this departure gate, and it is always rammed: sweaty, disgruntled passengers with too much hand luggage sinking pints and tipping back large glasses of wine. When you make it to the front you'll find your-self shoved up against the young Indian man you noticed earlier, standing by the window out onto the runway, tall and silent, not moving, just staring out at the lights of the planes on the wet tarmac, looking like he's in a different world entirely. Sorry, you'll say as you lurch into him, and he'll smile at you and say, in as broad a Belfast accent as any, No worries, you're grand. In an instant, he'll see that you are taken aback at his accent, and you'll see him see it, and he'll smile again, a smaller, tighter smile this time.

S'cuse me? the barman is saying to him. S'cuse me? Sir?

Pint of Guinness please, he'll say. From the beleaguered expression on the barman's face it's the hundredth time the poor man's had to explain that vouchers are not redeem-able against alcohol.

In that case what can we get? you'll hear yourself pipe up, a bit cheekily, overcompensating for the moment when you inadvertently betrayed yourself (you and them, us). The Belfastman will look at you, surprised, and then he'll grin, and the two of you will smile at each other as the barman lists the soft drinks available and finishes off with a litany of, salt 'n' vinegar, cheese 'n' onion or ready-salted crisps, KP Nuts, or bacon-flavoured scampi bites. Bacon-flavoured scampi bites! the Belfastman will shout in mock-incredulity. I've not had those since I was a child. Give us this much bacon-flavoured scampi bites, and he'll reach for your vouchers and thrust them, together with his, at the barman, who is not amused, and you will burst out laughing.

The slight acquaintance forged, he will offer to buy you a drink. Say yes. Don't even say yes, just don't say no. Hesitate, that will be enough.

By the curved brass railings at the edge of the bar area, you and Nirupam – that's his name, Nirupam Choudhury – will clink your glasses and start the customary dance of who-have-we-in-common? It will turn out that he grew up only a few streets away from you, in one of the big houses on Cyprus Avenue, and that you even attended, briefly, the same primary school.

Suddenly, a memory will surface: the shy skinny Paki kid and the two fat Chinky sisters being brought up onto the stage to celebrate Chinese New Year, and you'll feel yourself burn with embarrassment for him, for the school, for those words, and he'll see it all in your face and smile that tight sad smile again and say, Yep, that was me.

I'm sorry, you'll say, and he'll take a swig of his pint, then say, Look, don't worry about it.

In the short silence that follows you'll work out he was three years above you, and you'll find yourself blurting out, You don't remember my sister? Janey, you will say. Her name was Janey.

He'll start to shake his head, then stop, realise that you used the past tense, and he'll say, Not the Jane who died in P6? And then it'll be his turn to say, I'm sorry, and you'll say, like you always do, It's all right, and then you'll say, I was only six when Janey died, I don't even remember her myself, not really.

He'll look away then and say, My dad and baby sister died in a car accident the following year, and you'll realise with a start that this too sounds vaguely familiar. A special assembly, maybe, like there was for Janey, and the whole class signing a card. He was a surgeon, Nirupam will say, at the Royal Victoria, and after he died I used to hope my mum would move away, that we'd move back to England, but she never would.

He'll finish his pint and say, I did. I did as soon as I could.

Me too, you'll say, and then you'll hear yourself saying, I don't even remember anything about Janey, not really. Anything I do remember comes from photos. Photos, and my parents' stories. There's nothing of my own.

She gave me her packet of crisps, once, he'll say. I've never forgotten that. His eyes will light up at the memory. No one wanted to sit beside me, or talk to me in the playground, but she did, and she shared her packet of crisps.

Oh right, you'll say, trying to feign enthusiasm, because it can't have been Janey. Your mum worked at a dietician's, and she would never have allowed either of you crisps for break. But it will hardly seem worth pointing that out, and, besides, you won't want to break the moment.

You'll get a round in, and the two of you will stay talking until the flight – over four hours late by this time – is finally called, and in the scrum of boarding you'll manage to sit together, and you'll carry on talking all the way to Belfast, and all the time you wait at the luggage carousel, and all the way to the exit.

When you walk down the shabby carpet whose Welcome to Belfast messages woven in four or five languages have always seemed tired and grudging, or ironic, Nirupam will proclaim in a ridiculous accent, Wilkommen an Belfast!, and it will seem as if there's never been a better joke, and the two of you will laugh until you find yourself crying. Here, he'll say, and he'll touch your arm. It's okay.

I know, you'll say, blowing your nose. I'm sorry. Look at the state of me. It's just, you know.

I know, he'll say.

This is what you will have talked about. You will have told him how you've always felt lonely. You will have told him how they explained in Sunday school that those we'd lost watch over us, and how it was meant to comfort but instead terrified you, the thought of Janey at your shoulder following your every move, knowing your every thought. You will have told him that for a long time you weren't sure where she finished and you began. You only started liking books because of Janey. She had hundreds of books because she'd spent so long ill in bed with nothing to do but read, and you inherited them all, and first you read out of guilt, and then you read out of loneliness, and then you read because it had become a habit. Now you're an editorial assistant at a small publishing house, and you know your parents wonder, although they'd never say it, if that's what Janey would have done.

He will have told you how he too tried to make up to his mother for the loss of his father and sister — his father the top surgeon, his sister who hadn't had the chance to be or do anything and so who to his mother was everything. He couldn't do it: dropped out of medical school in his third year, took almost a year before plucking up the courage to tell his mother he'd done so. He's a sports journalist now, and she's too proud of him, clips out his newspaper articles and pastes them into a scrapbook, buys multiple copies to show to her friends so the originals don't get dog-eared. He will have told you too, a little bashfully, about the book he's writing in his spare time, a book about a young boy from Delhi growing up in Belfast who rides his bike along Cyprus Avenue. All of a sudden you will have remembered a time when they thought Janey was better and your parents bought the two of you new bicycles and you rode them all afternoon and into the dusk and you watched your big sister race ahead of you, swerving in and out of view between the trees on Cyprus Avenue.

You will realise, then, that you haven't forgotten entirely: that she's still there, inside of you, this something of her that's yours and yours only, and now that Nirupam's brought it back, no one can ever take the memory away, and you know how to remember her, and that's why you'll be laughing and crying at the silly shabby carpet too.

On the spur of the moment, as you are walking through the sliding glass doors of the arrivals hall into the frosty night, you will invite Nirupam Choudhury and his mother over to your parents' house for mulled wine the following day, Christmas Eve. As soon as you've said it, you will wonder if you've made a mistake, and what your parents will say, or whether or not Nirupam and his mother will even come. But when you say to your parents that you've invited them, it will turn out that your mum remembers Anjali Choudhury: they used to go to the same Mothers and Toddlers in the church hall of Bloomfield Presbyterian. Imagine, she'll say, her eyes brighter than you've seen them in years. Imagine, when our Janey and he were toddlers together.

On Christmas Eve, your father will light a fire in the living room, and the five of you will sit around it drinking mulled wine and eating the mince pies that Mrs Choudhury baked herself. You'll talk about Janey, of course, and Mr Choudhury, and Nisha. But you'll talk of other things too, of London, and books, and the way Belfast's changing.

You'll feel sheepish when the conversation turns to Belfast. Nirupam is more dutiful than you and comes back often. You come back to Belfast once a year, for Christmas and Boxing Day – Janey's Day – in one fell swoop, then back to London again on the twenty-seventh. But now, for the first time ever, you'll allow yourself to think that maybe you'll come back again in a few months' time, when the days are beginning to lengthen. You'll walk down Cyprus Avenue and all the streets you used to play on, Sandford Avenue and Sunbury Avenue and Evelyn Avenue and Kirkliston Drive, and maybe you'll walk on, walk the length of the Upper Newtownards Road, and the Albertbridge Road, and pause on the Albert Bridge itself, unlovely as it is, the traffic, the down-at-heel leisure centre, the railway station, to watch the starlings that mass and swoop above the east of the city in the evenings.

You'll catch Nirupam's eye, then, as if he's been reading your mind.

Christmas will be quiet, as always, but it will be a calm sort of quiet, this year, and for once you won't feel ridiculous, the three of you sitting in the cold dining room wearing paper hats while your father carves the turkey and your mother doles out the vegetables and you chatter in bursts about silly, inconsequential things.

Multitudes

VISITATIONS

THE CONSULTANT COMES INTO THE ROOM with eight or nine others. We are so new to this, barely twenty-four hours new, we don't yet know what this augurs. With the consultant is the registrar and two SHOs, the senior nurse and the other nurses and even the student nurse who knelt beside me at 3 a.m. last night and told me how her new-born son was premature and had to spend the first six weeks of his life in hospital. Our son is a full-term baby of nine days old, and we're still hoping this is nothing serious, a little bug, a false alarm. After the momentary comfort, I felt ashamed. I catch her eye now and smile, and she smiles back but is the first to look away although it's only later, much later, that I remember this because right now and without any preamble the consultant has started talking, and the first words she's said are, It's not good news.

PLATITUDES

Words don't fail us. The problem is the opposite: there are too many words. Too many words with too many syllables. There are also words we wish there weren't, these words in particular. Fifty per cent.

NUMBERS GAMES

Fifty per cent. Fifty-fifty. Heads or tails. Yes or no. We look at each other and say it with horror: fifty-fifty. But as the hours accumulate (two, three, twelve, twenty-four, thirty-six) and his temperature still won't come under control, we start to say it with a desperate sort of hope. Fifty-fifty. We'll take that. There's also 'half of all survivors'. We'll take that too. We'll take anything. We read and re-read the leaflet the consultant left us with, which isn't even really a leaflet, just five smudged and increasingly dog-eared photocopied pages stapled together in the left-hand corner. We read it hoping there's a paragraph or sentence or statistic we missed. There never is.

HE IS SO YOUNG WE DON'T EVEN KNOW YET WHAT COLOUR HIS EYES ARE GOING TO BE.

THE KINGDOM OF THE WELL AND THE KINGDOM OF THE SICK

In the darkest hours of the night, which aren't actually dark at all but punctured by the red and green glow of machines and the flashing yellow numbers and the strip lighting from the corridor and the bright lights of the nurses' station outside, my panicking mind, plundering its reservoirs, throws up all sorts of flotsam and jetsam, disconnected images and half-phrases half-remembered, a desperate attempt to make sense of things. The kingdom of the well and the kingdom of the sick is a phrase from – it comes to me – a Susan Sontag essay that I read as a student; somehow I've retained that much, although I haven't read the essay in question for years. The words go round and round in my mind, like the refrain from a catchy pop song lodged. The kingdom of the well and the kingdom of the sick. It's true: we have crossed a border. When people phone us from the distant lands of their own lives, their voices are tinny, distorted; there is a time lapse on the line that's not just the hospital's patchy reception. Over the past couple of days those closest to us have learned our new vocabularies and try them out with clumsy tongues. How are his temps, his obs, his bloods. Ceftriaxone, Nystatin. Recannulate. IV push. We are acquiring new vocabularies at a rapid pace, strings of acronyms and shorthands – GBS, PCR, LP. Some of these are almost familiar from teenage years spent watching *ER*. Get me an EKG and a Chem-7. Ninety over sixty and falling. Clear. When the doctors use a word we don't understand, we nod, and then, when they're gone, we google it. New immigrants to this land, we don't want to admit our weaknesses, our failings. We will master this language and in doing so we will wrest back control. Systolic, diastolic, pulse/ox, stat. Or maybe it's not that at all. Maybe the hope is that if we learn this new language, if we abide by the rules of this foreign land, keep our heads down and be thankful and eager and subservient, then one day we will be allowed to go home, or else we will blend in until we can slip back unnoticed over the border.

MOTHER'S MILK

He is too weak to feed and so I feed him a drop at a time, hour after hour, drop after drop after drop on the tip of my little finger. Then I express milk into a syringe and squeeze half a millilitre at a time into the corner of his flaccid mouth. Some of it he manages to swallow; most just dribbles away. I miss, even through the new mother's pain of cracked and bleeding nipples, his hot, sugary little mouth, the urgency of his latch, the pinching tug of his feeding. My breasts are swollen and hot with useless milk, the skin taut and shiny with angry red patches. I hook myself up to a hospital-grade pump and press the button to drain the milk out of me, my nipples swelling to raspberries. The little yellow-lidded bottles line up; all the milk he should be – isn't – getting. I've always thought 'nursing' a coy term for feeding a baby, a euphemism to avoid saying 'breasts'. But now I understand it. I am looking after my son in the only way I can, nursing him better one drop of milk at a time, hoping that everything the baby books say about the miraculous properties of breast milk is true. When they say I will have to stop feeding him while they analyse my breast milk to make sure I'm not infecting him through it I want, momentarily, and before I am ashamed of the thought and its despicable self-indulgence, to die.

WHERE HAVE ALL THE FLOWERS GONE?

It seems to have become the song I sing to him, rocking him in my arms to sleep. Sometimes I have to sing it several times before he succumbs and so we go round and around and around, the young men becoming soldiers becoming graveyards becoming flowers over and over, generation after generation of them. Just a few miles from our window people are pushing ceramic poppies on wire stalks into the ground around the Tower of London, commemorating the hundred-year dead. That world feels as far from us here and now as those old dead young men do. Sometimes I go on singing long after he's finally slipped into sleep, limp and heavy in my arms, the monitor wires and IV drips arranged carefully across the tight white sheets of his cot and fed into the glut of incessant beeping machines. I sing over the noise of the machines, and I sing myself into a sort of daze. Sometimes I try to sing alternative endings for the soldiers (Where have all the soldiers gone? They've all stopped fighting, every one), but nothing I invent will break for long the cycle of graveyards and flowers, flowers and graveyards. Sometimes I try to sing other songs. But I find I can't remember the words to 'Blowin' in the Wind' or 'My Grandfather's Clock', or even my own childhood favourite, 'Down by the Lock Hospital'. 'Puff the Magic Dragon' works for a while but then is too lurchingly sad: dragons live for ever, it goes, but not so little boys. My mouth is suddenly dry and my throat is cracked, and I go back to the flowers, no less sad, really, but blessedly meaningless, now, the hundredth time round.

DAYS

The days pass. We lose count of them. Someone asks if we would like to speak to the hospital chaplain. We say no, and so he (she?) never comes, but something about the offer – the combination of doctors and priests, perhaps – makes me think of the Larkin poem. I google it, and it is shorter than I remember. We no longer live in days. We live in an endless present tense that's both day and night and somehow neither, demarcated by obs every four hours, different drug cycles every four, six, eight and twenty-four, the combinations meeting and receding in an elegant quadrille. We save his nappies to be collected by the nurses and weighed. We roll them up into fat little bundles and line them up on paper towels, the time neatly written on the top right-hand corner, and we note their frequency and contents in a log chart. We keep feeding charts too: which side, how long, with what degree of vigour. These days are a particular time outside of time, like the air in the negative-pressure room, suspended, cut-off, an endless turning in on itself. Darkly, as much as we long for time to begin again, we hope that it won't, because its beginning again could mean the other of two things.

PERSONALITY

Here are the things we know about him. He hates his cot. He wriggles and writhes and thrashes and cries and stiffens his little back flat as a board until we pick him up and I lay him on my stomach, mewling and hiccuping, until he falls asleep. His cot, its bars painted blue and bright green, is called 'Inspiration', and it is where people do painful things to him, though they all tell us he is too young to make the association. I don't believe them. He knows. I know he knows. Other things we know about him. His smell and the particular warm heft of him, the feeling of his rapid hot little breaths against our chests or into our necks and his shuddering exhales, and the way his arms fling up above his shoulders in abandon when he sleeps and his drawn-up, froggy little legs. These are things every parent knows, but they are also specific to him, to us, as if we are the first in the world ever to know them. Other things. He has, somehow, at just a week and a half and against all the odds, begun to smile. We know the doctors will say this is impossible, say it is wind, or involuntary movement of the muscles, and so we document it furiously, tapping series of pictures into our phones, taking videos, before we look at each other and put down our phones and just smile back at him, eyes thick with tears. Yes, we say, that's right. Yes. Other things. We loved him as soon as he was born, bashed up and purple and battle-scarred, and we loved him fiercely and surprisingly, and what we said to him and to each other was, It's you, because it was him, and it had been all along, and it made such sense, that heady overwhelming flush of recognition. Other things. We knew he was unwell. We knew. Even without a rash or a temperature or any of the leaflet's other signs, we knew he wasn't himself, and we pushed for a second opinion, and this, and the brief hours it won us, might be what spares him.

PERIPHERAL VENOUS CANNULATION

When we were admitted it took three doctors six attempts to cannulate him, and eventually they had to bring up special equipment from Neonatal, a lightbox to shine through his veins, which were too thin to be seen by the naked eye. The cannula lasted a day before the vein gave up and the whole procedure needed to be done again. It's been redone three times now: his veins collapsing one after another under the intensity and duration of the IV drugs. He's had the right hand, the left, the right again, the left foot. This time there is talk of them putting the cannula into his scalp, and we recoil and say, Please, no, please. We look at his scalp, and we see the juicy veins just under the surface, and we say, Please, only as a last resort. The nurse says, If they have to do it that way they'll give him a little cap to wear, it will be okay, you won't see anything. We kiss his hands and feet and forehead and cry, both of us, and then we leave the room before the doctors begin, but we hear his cries the length of the corridor and until we've put two double doors between us. My own left hand is still aubergine from a failed attempt to cannulate me during his birth. I run the fingertips of my right hand over the bruise and then press down as hard as I can.

THE REASONS (WE TELL HIM) TO STAY IN THIS WORLD

During my – our – protracted labour, I tell him, I used (too much and incorrectly) gas and air and went temporarily crazy, although I thought I was perfectly lucid at the time. I started stamping and swaying from side to side and chanting in a deep, loud, atonal voice and in between contractions explained to my husband, politely, patiently, and in my normal voice that I was in the middle of a shamanic rite, calling the spirit of our unborn child from where it was roaming on the plains, telling him – we didn't know the gender, but I already knew it was a him – that the time had come to be born. I tell our son this now, how I called his spirit into this world, and I tell him that I will fight for it against the forces that want to suck it back. My husband lists all of the containers – our word for them, an obscure joke whose origins we can't now remember – that we have bought to put him in and keep him safe. His car seat. His Bednest cot. His Sleepyhead pillow. His Moby wrap. His BabyBjörn bouncer. His baby bath with its moulded sponge insert. His highchair with a newborn attachment. There are half a dozen of them, a dozen. My husband reaches the end of the list and begins again, a litany. We tell him it's a beautiful world. The cheap pocket radio is talking of Gaza and Ebola and Operation Yewtree and global warming, and we look at each other and tell him, as parents must have murmured to newborns for decades, centuries, that it's his job now to make the world better. At some point we stop giving reasons and just tell him, Stay.

FICTION

For the first time in my life, fiction has failed me. I can't imagine myself out of myself, or even imagine doing so. One evening, when I am so exhausted I can't imagine how I'll last through another night, my husband offers to read to me. He picks up a magazine and opens it at random and reads a review of a new restaurant in Brooklyn. It is the first time in our lives that he has ever read to me. Between sentences, perhaps even between words, I dip in and out of sleep. Our son is lying in the crook of my husband's left arm, naked but for a nappy, limbs limp, mouth open. My husband reads, self-conscious. I have never loved him as much as I love him then. He turns a page and reads his way through a poem, stumbling slightly. The poem is a son's memories of his father, a lifeguard, and the one time he saved people from drowning. It moves from concrete memories to abstract musings, from the people saved and lost that day to the sky above and the ceaselessly moving

waves. Read it again, I say when he finishes, and after that,
And again?

MULTITUDES

Before we are born, we decide in advance the lives we are
going to live, the events in them, the people, the choices.
We decide according to the lessons we want to learn, and
all of us have lived here many times over, learning new and
different lessons, meeting over and over the same people in
endlessly new configurations. I dream this in the light hot
daze of one snatched nap, in the sweat of the faux-leather
chair-bed and the stiff, faded cellular blankets, and for a few
minutes when I wake it all makes sense and the ancient
wisdom in my baby's grave and luminous eyes is obvious,
and I think, *You're here to teach me too*, and for a moment I
even have a fleeting grasp of the lesson.

HOMEWARD

And then, almost as quickly as it started, it is over: we are
being told his clinical signs are good, they've been stable
for forty-eight hours now and so we can go home – they
need the room, and we live near and can bring him in
three times a day to receive the rest of the course of his
IV drugs. So we are suddenly packing a week's worth of
accumulated things: a cheap supermarket duvet and my
breastfeeding pillow, energy bars and packets of dried fruit,
crumpled clothes and toothbrushes and the pocket-sized

radio, unread magazines and tubes of nipple cream, pil-
ing everything haphazard into the plastic laundry sacks
the nurses have given us because we don't have any other
bags. Then we're leaving the room and walking the length
of the ward and through the double doors and along the
corridors and into the lift and down and through more
corridors, through the main reception and into the concrete and litter of a Whitechapel afternoon, the knots of
smokers and the traffic fumes, the flapping tarpaulins of
the fish and vegetable stalls across the road and the racks
of flimsy fluttering chiffon outside the sari shops. My husband has gone home every night to sleep and has been to
and from the supermarket on errands, and he strides on
ahead carrying the baby in his car seat, but my legs are
wobbly. I've been out of the hospital – out of our son's
room, in fact – only twice in seven days, when it all got
too much and I walked through the corridors and took the
lift down to the entrance hall to stand in the sunlight with
the smokers and cry. It feels too soon to be going home.
It seems as if they've only just told us how seriously ill he
is. Fifty-fifty. We are the first fifty, or the second, the right
fifty. It's chance, luck, Alexander Fleming in 1928, nothing
we've done, and this makes us fearful. The ferocity I felt
through the nights in hospital, the conviction that I could
and would fight for his soul, has melted away in the day-
light, and now it's just the three of us, left to watch and wait
and muddle through. Wait for me, I say, suddenly terrified,
and I heave the laundry sack over my shoulder. We have to
stay together. We have to. That's all there is.

STORYTELLING

He's too young to remember any of it, they say. He won't remember a thing. We think of his eyes in pain, black with incomprehension and fear and bewilderment, and we are not so sure, and we agree more out of politeness even than hope. He is talking to himself as I write this. Gurgles, coos, the occasional indignant squawk. Heh-gooo, haw. Uh-heh, glaaaaa. Eoow. Batting with his right hand, now finally out of its cumbersome bandage, a green bird with rattling beads in its tummy suspended from a loop on the playmat he lies on. He is utterly absorbed. Ah-gooo, haw. Heh-eoow. Are you telling a story? I ask him, as I kneel down beside him. He looks up at me, beams his gummy little grin, and even as I smile back at him and rub his fat little stomach my own stomach lurches. *It will always be like this*, I think. But perhaps it always is. Sometimes he smiles as he is sleeping, and sometimes he sucks down imaginary milk. Sometimes his tiny face creases and his chin quivers and he cries out his distress cry. Then we rush to pick him up, but even by the time our hands are around the soft heavy warmth of his swaddled body he is gone again, the memory, if that is what it was, already, at least momentarily, forgotten.

Acknowledgements

I would like to thank the various editors who have helped with individual stories in this collection: Liz Allard, Ellah Allfrey, Brendan Barrington, Sinéad Gleeson, Heather Larmour, Adrian McKinty, Deirdre Madden and Stuart Neville. Thanks are also due to Mike Brett, Carlo Gébler, Sarah Hall, Leo Mellor, Rowan Routh, Damian Smyth, Di Speirs and last, but perhaps most of all, Joe Thomas.

I am very grateful to Van Morrison for allowing me to use his lines from 'Astral Weeks' as the collection's epigraph, and my debt to him exceeds these lines: as a Belfast writer, and a writer of and from the east, not just my city but my imagination too have been formed and shaped by his lyrics. Thanks also to Colin Dundas of Exile Productions.

Thank you to Peter Straus at Rogers, Coleridge & White, to Liz Hudson at The Little Red Pen for her scrupulous copy-editing and to everyone at Faber, especially Kate McQuaid and Luke Bird for his beautiful cover design. The biggest thank you of all to my wonderful editor, Angus Cargill, who has worked on these stories with me for years, when the collection was little more than a handful of sparks and wishful thinking.

Thank you to my parents and to my sisters, who have enjoyed (and sometimes endured) my stories for almost exactly three decades now.

And finally to Tom, for everything.